THE SPACE BETWEEN HERE & NOW

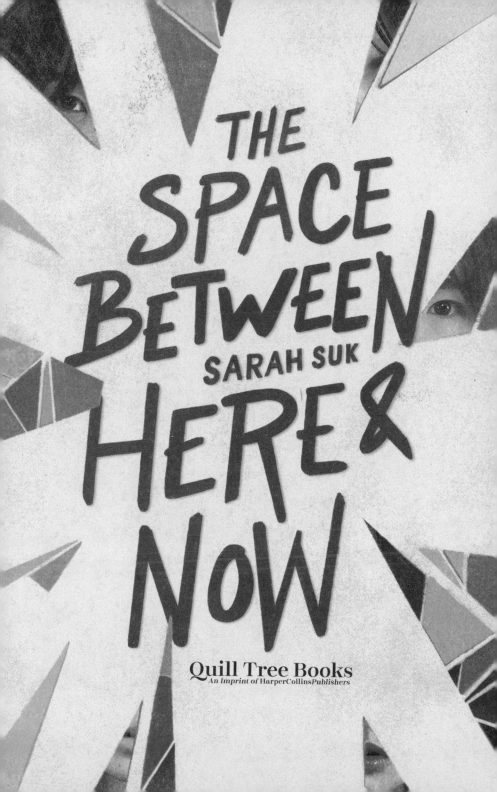

THE SPACE BETWEEN

SARAH SUK

HERE & NOW

Quill Tree Books
An Imprint of HarperCollins Publishers

For Sue O, the one who grounds me in the present
and the one who makes it glow.

One

I t's not easy explaining what it feels like to disappear in ten words or less.

The closest way I can describe it is the feeling of walking up the stairs in the dark—maybe in the middle of the night when you're on your way back to bed after using the bathroom or stumbling home from a party, too drunk to find the light switch—and thinking there's one less step than there is. Your foot plummets through thin air, your stomach goes with it, and in my case, the rest of your body follows.

There one second. Gone the next.

But that's not ten words, and ten words max is all I have with Appa before he starts to get that look in his eye, the look that says, *I'm here but not really here.* He does that a lot. Goes to this place inside his head where I can't follow.

I lie on my bed, fully dressed, 7:07 a.m., practicing how I want to tell him what I want to tell him in a way that'll make him listen. Really listen. I've been thinking about it since yesterday, when Disappearance Number Nine happened. "He's your dad," Nikita reminded me. "Of course he'll listen."

Easy for Nikita to say. She has breakfast every Sunday with her own dad, eating scones spread with their home-made blueberry jam. Nikita's my best friend and I love her, but I also know Appa. I close my eyes, try to picture us making jam together.

Impossible. My brain literally can't compute it.

I go back to counting words on my hands, fingers going up and then back down like I'm mapping out the syllables of a haiku. But I'm not trying to write poetry. I'm just trying to figure out a way to talk to my dad.

"Appa, I need to tell you . . . No, no. So, funny story! Wait, no. No useless intros. Straight to the point, Aimee, straight to the point."

I recite until at last, I think I've got it. I roll out of bed and strap my film camera over my shoulder, grab my back-pack, palms sweaty, and head to the kitchen.

He's sitting at the table, already deep in his weekday morning ritual when I walk in. Coffee in the same green mug with the spider crack along the handle, scrolling through the news on his phone, eating a bowl of cereal. Today it's Special K, the vanilla almond kind. Our pantry is full of cereal boxes (courtesy of Appa), arranged by box color (courtesy of me). My mom used to call it our cereal library. It's one of the few things that hasn't changed since she left.

"Morning, Aimee," he says, not looking up from his phone.

I jump straight to it, not wasting time.

"It happened again yesterday."

His fingers pause over his screen. He looks up.

In his face, I see my own thick eyebrows, round nose, slightly crooked mouth. People always say how much I look like my dad. *You are your father's daughter!* The expression in his eyes, though, is unreadable. Concern, maybe? Yes, actually, he does look kind of worried. He's sitting straighter now, more attentive. A balloon of hope rises in my chest. He's listening.

"You vanished?" he asks.

We speak in a mix of English and Korean, but he says this word in Korean.

Sarajyeosseo?

I nod.

"When? At school?"

"Lunchtime. For two minutes."

Damn it. I've gone off script from what I practiced, and I realize too late that I've used up all my words. Almost as if on cue, Appa's shoulders relax and his eyes drift back to his phone.

"Okay. Two minutes is nothing. Good thing you didn't miss any of your classes."

The balloon in my chest pops.

Untrue, by the way. Two minutes is not nothing. In that time, you can make a cup of tea. Meet the love of your life. Take a photo. No, fifty photos. In two minutes, you can disappear in the middle of having lunch with your best

3

friend on the school bleachers and end up traveling back in time, stuck in a memory until you're sent back to where you belong like a tennis ball being lobbed back and forth between the present and the past.

"It's not nothing," I say. My voice clips with frustration. "This is the third time this year it's happened, and I never disappear this often." I swallow hard, knuckles going white around my backpack straps. "I need help. I think we should look into a specialist."

The words drop between us, heavy. He looks up again and for the briefest of seconds, I think I've gotten through to him. There's a flicker of acknowledgment on his face, a shutter lens opening to see the light. But then he smiles in a way that's meant to be reassuring and says, "I told you, Aimee. You'll grow out of it one day. You're only, what—seventeen? This is a phase. You don't need a specialist. In the meantime, you have to try harder not to give in to the temptation. Okay?"

I open my mouth, but nothing comes out. Maybe it's because I've surpassed my word limit.

Snapshot: Appa and me, locked in a staring contest. Coffee steam, refrigerator hum, the alphabet shriveling up in my brain. Nothing but sand in my head, stretching for miles and miles.

"Now, aren't you going to eat?" He nods at the table, where he's set out an empty bowl and spoon for me, next to the carton of 2 percent milk.

My frustration builds into anger, pressing against the hollow of my throat. Is this how he's going to end the conversation? I consider walking out right now in protest, turning my back on both him and my cereal bowl, maybe even slamming the door on my way out so he'll *have* to pay attention and take me seriously.

But he looks so hopeful, like he's saying, *Please. Let's just get back to our morning routine. Cereal and silence. Like father, like daughter, right?*

No matter how disappointed I feel, I don't want to disappoint Appa too. Something in me rejects it, would rather embrace the sand in my mind than choose to see disappointment on his face. So I let it go and drop my backpack on the floor, grab a box of Rice Krispies from the pantry and shake it into my bowl, motions jerky, kernels falling over the edge. My anger fizzles, or at least gets pressed deep down, muffled and quiet.

"Everything will be okay," Appa says.

After that, we fall back into silence, punctuated only by the snap, crackle, pop of my breakfast cereal.

I was born with Sensory Time Warp Syndrome. Sounds like some kind of sci-fi experiment gone wrong, but in reality, it's a rare condition that makes you physically travel back in time to certain memories when exposed to trigger senses linked with that memory. At least, that's what the pamphlet that I received when I was nine told me. That was the first and last time I ever went to go see a doctor about it. "The root cause is unknown," he said at the time. "But many people grow out of it. There's a good chance you will too."

For me, my trigger sense is always smell. That means that when I smell something related to a memory, I go right back in time to that moment. Not every time, mind you. It's unpredictable when exactly it'll happen. One second I'm in the present, and the next, I disappear mid-sentence, mid–sandwich bite, mid–whatever the hell I was in the middle of doing, and I'm in the past. Once the memory is over, I get snapped right back to the present.

Sometimes, like yesterday, I'm gone for two minutes. The longest I've ever been gone was ten minutes.

Appa clung on to the doctor's words like a life raft. He's been calling it a phase ever since, reminding me that it's only a matter of time until I grow out of it. For a long time, I believed him. The disappearances were infrequent enough that it was easy to chalk them up as little inconveniences. But these days, with me disappearing more often, I've started wondering. What happens if I don't grow out of it? What happens if this is a forever thing?

It's drizzling when I jog out of the apartment. I pull up the hood of my rain jacket, shielding my camera with one hand as I scan the street for Nikita. A second later I see her turning the corner in her red Mini Cooper, honking the horn with a grin.

This car is her pride and joy. Her parents gave it to her

when she passed her novice driver's test earlier this year, and she affectionately named it Twizzlers. I don't know when I'll get a driver's license of my own. The thought of vanishing in the middle of driving and causing some kind of terrible accident has stopped me from even taking the written learner's test. Not to mention, people with STWS need an official doctor's note with a stamp of approval in order to drive, and I can't think of any doctor who would give me a thumbs up to get behind the wheel with all my recent disappearances. But generous soul that Nikita is, she picks me up on her way to school every morning. I climb into the passenger seat, grateful to be inside. The rain's coming down harder now. Typical Vancouver, kicking off March with one downpour after another.

"Good morning," Nikita says. She's wearing an orange sundress with wedge sandals because weather be damned, Nikita Lai-Sanders will always dress like it's the middle of summer. "How'd the talk with your dad go?"

"Good morning. And fine." I snap my seat belt on, maybe a little too aggressive.

She raises an eyebrow. "Fine as in fine or fine as in FINE?"

Fine is fine. FINE, in all caps, is our acronym for Falling Into Never-ending Emptiness. A bit dramatic maybe, but we were twelve when we thought of it and considered ourselves geniuses.

"All caps," I sigh.

"Ah." Nikita shoots me a quick sympathetic look as

she drives. "He didn't listen? Even after you told him what happened yesterday?"

"I could barely tell him anything, to be honest."

She shakes her head, in sync with the windshield wipers. "I don't get it. If I was traveling back in time, my parents would want to know everything. What was the memory? Were they in it? How did they look? Et cetera et cetera."

"Well, you know my dad," I say.

She pauses. "I don't, actually. All I know about him is that I should call him Mr. Roh and that he's way younger than my dad. He's like forty or something, right?"

"Thirty-six this year, I think."

"My parents both just turned fifty-seven and they're always like, 'Wow, Aimee's dad, so young.' But honestly, other than that, your dad's kind of a mystery."

I don't know what to say to that. Nikita's looking at me like she's waiting for me to offer more details. Instead, I turn on the radio.

"Well, your dad might not be curious about where you go back to, but if you ever want to talk about it . . ." Nikita throws me a smile. "I'm here for you."

"Thanks." I smile back. It's not that I don't trust Nikita. If there was anyone in the world I would talk to about the memories I visit, it would be her. I've already told her about a few of them—like Disappearance Number Four, the time I revisited the moment we first became friends, in grade six when we were partnered together for a papier-mâché art project on whales (scent: Elmer's glue and newspaper); or Disappearance Number Three, the summer vacation I spent in Korea when I was seven, eating hoddeok with the first boy I ever had a crush on, a family friend's son who liked to draw pretend tattoos on himself (scent: cinnamon and honey). I let him draw a pear on my wrist and I wouldn't erase it for weeks. Nikita still likes to tease me about that one to this day.

The thing is, it's easier to talk about some memories than others. I haven't really figured out how to talk about all of them yet. Especially the one I went back to yesterday.

Nikita clears her throat. "Also, just a reminder that if you ever go back to our first year of high school, please, please stop me from dating David. He's texting me again. Dude can't take a hint."

"It's not like that. You know I can't change anything." I can't even interact with anyone in my memories. I just appear like a ghost, invisible to everyone, stuck watching the scene play out like a movie until it's time to go back. It definitely takes the potential fun out of time traveling when you can't engage with anything. All those time travel movies make it look way cooler than it actually is.

"Just keep it in mind. For if the rules ever change," she says.

"Block David at all costs. Got it." I nod. "So why's he been texting you anyway?"

"Ugh, don't get me started," Nikita says before launching into it.

9

I lean back in my seat, only half listening. My mind is wandering now, thinking over my conversation with Appa from this morning and what Nikita just said. *For if the rules ever change.*

Honestly? I'm not even sure what the rules are. I smell certain things, I disappear, I come back. Time moves on while I'm gone, so whatever I miss in the present, I can never get back.

Everything I know about Sensory Time Warp Syndrome, I learned from the pamphlet, the internet, and a small online forum I discovered a few years back with other people diagnosed with STWS. There was also that one Vancouver meetup I went to last year, though that wasn't as helpful as I thought it would be. But other than that, the resources I've had have always felt like enough. But now . . . I lean my head against my palm, feeling restless, thinking back to that first doctor's appointment when I was nine. I had blood tests, X-rays, full-body examinations. "Totally healthy, no abnormalities," the doctor said. "And yet."

And yet.

"I've never met anyone with this condition myself," the doctor said. His gaze flickered to Appa. "If we could speak privately about the possibility of Aimee coming in for some studies at the hospital . . ."

"No," Appa said flatly. "No one is doing tests on my daughter."

"Oh no, Mr. Roh, it's not what you're thinking. It would

be studies to help us understand the nature of the condition better than we currently do. Nothing invasive. And any studies we conduct would be with your consent, of course."

But Appa wouldn't hear of it. He stood up, taking my hand. "You said there's a good chance children grow out of it?"

"Well, yes. In the cases I've read about—"

"That's all we need to know. We can handle this on our own, thank you."

And that was that.

I wonder if things might have been different if I had gone in for those studies. At that point, I had only vanished once. Could I have stopped the eight other times if I had done more work then? Not that I would have been able to without Appa's permission. Or my mom's, if she'd still been around then.

"—so you'll be there, right? The grad auction?" Nikita's urgent voice brings me back to the moment. I sit up straighter, trying to piece together what I missed. "I need backup. David's definitely going to try to corner me there."

Okay. I'm pretty sure she's talking about the auction after school today. The grad committee is putting it on as a fundraiser. I nod. "Sure. I'll be there. You know no one sets up chairs better than me."

She grins. "Good. Make sure not to disappear on me, okay?"

She says it like a joke, so I laugh, even though in my

head, all I'm thinking about is how FINE I feel.

I used to vanish once every year or two at most. But the fact that it's already happened three times in this new year alone . . . I mean, maybe it means nothing. Maybe I'm just getting it out of my system all in one go and I won't ever vanish again. But I can't help but worry, like something's not right.

Like my body's trying to tell me something.

If Appa's not going to take it seriously, I'm going to need to figure out a way to help myself.

One of the most difficult aspects for those who live with STWS is how seemingly random their condition can be. No two people experience it the same, and even for a single individual, a trigger that sends them back to a memory one day may not have the same effect the next. This can make it challenging to know what triggers to avoid. Even so, it could be helpful for people with STWS to make note of their known triggers in order to detect any possible patterns, or at the very least, to keep a recorded history of their condition.

Two

Nikita and I always go to school an hour early. She's vice president of the student council, chair of the grad committee, and self-appointed member at large of the debate team. "Can you appoint yourself as member at large?" I had asked, to which she replied, "Aimee. It's Wilson Oak Secondary's debate team. You can do anything and they won't argue with you." Probably explains why our debate team hasn't won any competitions in the past decade.

She has meetings every morning. Me? I go to the dark-room.

My photography teacher, Ms. Ferris, always comes to school early and opens up the art room for any students who want to use it before the first bell, as long as we clean up after ourselves. She's sweet, Ms. Ferris. She speaks in the softest voice, the kind you have to pay attention to otherwise you might entirely miss what she's saying. She's an art teacher by day and a kickboxing instructor by night. So basically, sweet and also kind of badass. It's hard some-times to picture her getting pumped up and yelling in a fitness class, but as she always reminds us, our art contains multitudes and so do we.

A few other students are already in the art room when I get there. It's busier than usual for this time, and then it hits me—the auction tonight. A bunch of our classmates are auctioning off their art for the grad fundraiser and I see some familiar faces putting the final touches on their pieces. Russell Shah looks up from his easel and waves at me.

"Hey, Paper Bag Princess," he says. "Here to make some last-minute changes like the rest of us?"

Paper Bag Princess. It's a nickname he's given me because of my choice of clothes: always neutral and always over-sized and cozy. White, black, gray, beige. I love beige. Some might call it boring, but is there anything more comforting than your favorite beige sweater tucked into a pair of white drawstring pants?

Appa says I look like I'm about to paint a room any time I wear this outfit. But I like to leave the color to the accessories. Clay earrings the shade of cherry Starbursts. A turquoise scarf, patterned with ocean waves. Today is a burnt-orange headband, sweeping the baby hairs off my forehead.

"Nah," I say. "I'm not submitting anything. Besides, I'm not a procrastinator like you. I would've finished long before the due date."

He cups a hand around his ear. "Hark. Is that hypocrisy I hear? No, wait, sounds more like a straight-up lie."

I laugh. Ever since we first started high school, Russell

and I have been in the same art class, and any time we had a project or presentation, we would 100 percent be Those Kids who were working on it until the second it was due. When I came running into the classroom to make my finishing touches, he would always be there too. His dream is to be a picture book illustrator.

Two years ago, he told me that he liked me and asked me to go to the spring dance with him, and I said no. It wasn't just because I wasn't sure if I liked him back in that way, but it was also the idea of going on my first date to a crowded dance. What if I vanished? There would be so many people, so many scents crowded into the school gymnasium, soda and sweat and heavy cologne. I didn't like the thought of that being my first date or my first dance, so I turned him down.

I still haven't been to a school dance. Or on a first date. But I'm grateful that Russell understood and that our friendship has stayed intact with no trace of awkwardness between us. He's dating someone else now, Jamie from AP Literature, and I couldn't be happier for him. I can't help but wonder, though, when it'll be my turn to have some firsts. When I'll start letting myself have a turn.

I step behind Russell and take a look at his painting. It's a whimsical scene of an anglerfish swimming through outer space, surrounded by planets. It's good. Beautiful, even. *Multitudes and multitudes*. I can definitely imagine it in a book one day.

"What do you think?" he asks, a hint of nervousness in his voice as he glances between me and the painting.

"Russ, you've done the impossible," I say decisively. "You've made an anglerfish look adorable. A true feat."

He grins. "Be serious."

"I am. Whoever wins this tonight is going to be a very lucky bidder." I place a hand against my heart. "Honest."

"Thanks. I'm still not sure about these planets, though. I was going for grand. Does it feel grand?"

"Very."

"I was also going for breathtaking."

"Consider my breath stolen."

He rolls his eyes, but I can see the pride flicker in his smile. "Really, though, why aren't you submitting anything? I bet you'd get some great bids on your photos."

I shrug lightly and start walking backward toward the darkroom. "I just don't have anything to showcase."

"Last few years tire you out?" he asks. "What happened to the Aimee Roh who was first in line for any opportunity to show off her work?"

"Figured I should try and share the spotlight," I joke, making finger guns at his painting. "Get it? Light? Anglerfish? The light on top of his head?"

"That's a stretch, Aimee."

I thought it was pretty good for something I just made up on the spot. I smile and wave, disappearing into the darkroom with a quick knock on the door to alert anyone on the other side. Though this door doesn't lead into the actual darkroom. Instead, it opens almost immediately to a second door, which then leads into the darkroom. The space between the doors is a buffer so people don't accidentally flood the darkroom with light when they walk in. I wait for the first door to close completely before stepping through the second door. It's empty inside.

I let out a heavy breath, my smile slipping as I think about what Russell said.

What happened to Aimee Roh?

I don't quite know what to say to that, which is part of the problem. When you display your work, people expect you to talk about it, and lately all I've been able to think about is what might happen if I vanish in the middle of sharing a photograph, everyone gaping at me like a magic trick. Like what happened last year.

Ms. Ferris was hosting an end-of-semester student art show and I, like I always did, jumped at the chance to participate. I had just completed a project re-creating stills from *Alice in Wonderland* and I was feeling proud of the way all my photos had turned out, printed large and crisp in frames on the wall. The turnout was great: students, teachers, family, friends. I had a bowl of candy set out for people who visited my gallery, prepared with a spiel on how I went about crafting my photo shoot.

It was all going well until I caught a whiff of someone's perfume as they leaned in to take a closer look at my photos.

It was so sudden. It always is. Grapefruit and musk, and then I was gone, vanishing in front of a crowd of people mid-sentence about my costume choices.

It was Disappearance Number Six: a short memory in a library from when I was a child, my mom reaching over me to grab a book from the top shelf. She wore this perfume, briefly, back when she was in a stage of experimenting with different fragrances. Our apartment always smelled like the new signature scent she was trying to emulate before she decided that none of the perfumes were quite *her* and got rid of them all, the smell of grapefruit the last to fade away, stubbornly clinging onto all her clothes until the very last moment.

When I returned a minute and a half later, nobody cared about my photos anymore, or what I had to say. All anyone wanted was to stare at me and bombard me with questions about what had just happened, some even asking me if I could do it again so they could catch it on video. Ms. Ferris quickly dispersed the crowd, rallying them away with a protective glare in her eyes. I could see her kickboxing energy shining through in that moment.

I'd never disappeared in front of an audience like that before, and thinking about it happening again makes me feel nauseous. Maybe I used to like sharing my work, but these days, I just want to keep my head down until I can figure out why I keep disappearing.

Sometimes it feels like talking to people, even people

I'm close to like Nikita or Russell, takes up all my energy. Especially these days when I have so much on my mind. I don't even realize how much effort I'm putting into holding up a smile, a laugh, a conversation, until I'm alone and I feel a sense of numbness drape itself over my chest like a weighted blanket. It's not that I'm pretending around other people. The smile is real. So's the laugh. But this feeling I fall back to when I'm quiet and alone is like returning to my default setting.

In the darkroom, though, that numb feeling lifts a bit, and a space opens up for me to breathe. Maybe because in here, I know I won't disappear. The smells are always the same. Chemicals, negative strips, scents that have never made me vanish and that I trust never will.

It's safe here.

I turn on the regular lights and prepare the chemicals, pouring the developer, stop bath, and fixer in individual trays, carefully lining up a pair of clean tongs against each one. After I set up my box of photo paper and folder of negative strips at one of the enlargers, I switch off the regular lights and turn on the safe light. The room goes dim and red, and I give my eyes a second to adjust before getting to work.

I first discovered film photography when I was eight years old, two years after my mom walked out on me and Appa without a word. No explanation, no goodbye. The only item she left behind was a Canon AE-1 film camera and I became fascinated with it. For a while, I just liked looking at it from afar, but then I learned how to actually use it through YouTube—loading the film, focusing the lens, how to set the aperture and shutter speed. Once I got to high school, I jumped at the chance to develop my own film in our school's photography elective.

I wonder if my mom printed her own photos too.

I wonder what she liked taking pictures of.

I'm not working on any particular project today. Lately, I've been coming to print random photos from my negatives, just to relax. I expose a square piece of glossy white photo paper with light from the enlarger and then take it to the developer tray, dropping it into the liquid.

This is my favorite part. Watching nothing become something.

The image slowly begins to emerge.

Snapshot of what I remember from this moment: Appa at work in the car shop. Grease and grime, the clatter of tools, a smudge across his face that made me smile because he felt closer in that moment, less distant, more real, with that streak of dirt right by his nose. It's just dirt. It's just grime. But there was something about it that tugged on my heart and stayed there.

Actual snapshot that appears on the paper: Appa peering into the open hood of a car, slightly out of focus, the name tag on his navy-blue mechanic uniform starting to peel off. James Roh, it says. His work name. His real name is Hyunwoo.

I stare at his face appearing in the developer. It wasn't always like this. This distance between us. The first time I disappeared, he dropped everything to pick me up at school as soon as the principal called to tell him what happened. He listened to every detail, how the smell of freshly baked bread that my teacher brought in sent me back to a time when we were standing in line for buns at Blue Bunny Bakery. There was a new weekly collectible sticker of the bakery's mascot in each package—a rabbit in a chef's hat shaped like bread—and Appa took me every Saturday morning because I wanted to collect them all.

He made a doctor's appointment immediately, the one where I learned that I had STWS and was told I would grow out of it soon enough. I'm not sure how we got here from where we used to be, from when he would come running when I needed him. The change happened so gradually that by the time I realized he didn't come running anymore, I had already forgotten how to talk to him.

What happened to Aimee Roh?

What happened to us?

I go through the rest of the darkroom steps, dropping the photo in the stop bath, then the fixer, then the wash, circling the square photo through running water, before hanging it up to dry just as the first bell rings.

The photo is too blurry to see the smudge on his face.

Three

I nearly make it through the whole day without being called into Mr. Riaga's office, but right after AP Literature, he catches me on my way to my locker, making his way through the crowded hallways with one finger in the air to grab my attention. You know, just in case I can't hear him bellowing my name down the hall.

"Aimee! Aimee Roh! If you have a moment . . . !"

My cheeks warm as everyone turns to look at me. He's a kind man, Mr. Riaga, but subtlety is not his strong suit. Ironic since he once told me that he prefers to call students into his office naturally rather than announcing it over the PA system so as not to draw unwanted attention. At least it's nice to have a school counselor who genuinely cares about his students, hallway yelling and all.

"I was hoping to run into you," he says, approaching me with a warm smile. "Do you have a moment to chat in my office?"

"Sure, Mr. Riaga," I say. "But you know it's technically not running into someone if you purposefully find them in the hallway and yell their name, right?"

"I have no idea what you mean."

I follow him to his office. I've been a regular here since I first started high school. Principal Keller wanted me to be well acquainted with our counselor, given my rare condition and my potential need for extra support (her words). After every one of my disappearances, Mr. Riaga has found me in the hallway to check in. Like I said, it's nice that he cares. Though honestly, I'm not sure how much it helps.

I take a seat in my usual spot across his desk, where he has a lineup of framed photos. I've pretty much got all the pictures memorized by now. Mr. Riaga with his wife and two daughters on a camping trip, a big group photo with extended family taken on one of his summer trips to Kenya, his soccer team holding up the first-place trophy they won in last year's men's league—that one's the newest desk photo. He was very proud to add that one.

"So, Aimee," he says, sitting down in his squeaky wheely chair. "Another disappearance yesterday, huh?"

"Who told you this time?" I ask.

"Nobody directly. But it's what I've been hearing."

My cheeks warm again. Right. People talk and word always gets around.

"Want to talk about it?"

"Not really."

He nods, understanding. "Okay. Just the bare facts then, so I can write them down for your file."

I sigh. "It was yesterday at lunch. School bleachers. I

was gone for two minutes."

He nods again, jotting this down on a notepad. "Were you with anyone?"

"Nikita. There were a couple others around too, eating lunch."

"Scent?"

I pause, yesterday's memory flashing through my mind. Something like nausea rolls through my stomach and my throat gets a little tighter; it's a little harder to breathe. I grip the edges of my chair, knuckles white, swallowing hard.

Mr. Riaga lowers his notepad.

"Aimee? Are you okay?"

I nod, even though I'm not sure if I am. Yesterday's memory is still so vivid in my mind.

I was six and my mom was gone. It was the first morning I'd ever woken up to an apartment without her. Memory Me followed the smell of cigarettes and oksusu cha to the kitchen, where Appa was sitting at the table, smoking, staring at nothing, the kettle on the stove rattling and clouded in steam.

I was six and my dad was gone. Not gone like my mom was, but gone in the way he's kept on disappearing ever since, slowly and slowly, more and more so. I could see it in his eyes, even then. If I had to point out the beginning of the change between us, it would be here.

"Appa?" Memory Me said.

He looked up and I saw the tears in his eyes. "Aimee,"

he said. The tears came loose, falling down his face. It was my first time seeing Appa cry.

There was nothing to fill the air but smoke and steam. Appa said he quit smoking after I was born, but on this day the ashtray in front of him was already full. Afterward, I never saw him smoke again, making this moment feel like a hazy dream. I didn't stay long enough to see who turned off the stove and I can't remember who eventually did. All I remember about the rest of the day is drinking corn tea, the faint taste of ashes on my tongue.

Mr. Riaga is staring at me, concerned. "You still with me, Aimee? Can you tell me about the scent?"

I exhale slowly through my nose. "Corn tea and cigarettes. I had the tea in my thermos and some kids were smoking under the bleachers."

Mr. Riaga hesitates and then writes it down. "Are you sure you don't want to talk about where you went back to?"

The nausea still lingers. It's never been this hard to talk about my disappearances before, and I've never been so on edge about it. *Two minutes is nothing.* That's what Appa said. And in some ways, maybe he's right. The memory was so short and so long ago, it should be easier to talk about than this. But the words lodge somewhere in my throat and won't come out. I take another breath, slow.

"Not yet. No."

"Okay."

Silence.

Mr. Riaga puts his notepad on the desk and folds his hands on top of it. "I've been doing some extra reading on STWS lately. Apparently, disappearances can increase if you're under more stress. Would you say that's been the case for you?"

Oh. I'm touched that Mr. Riaga has been doing his own research on STWS. It's not often that people do that. Usually if they have questions, they'll ask me about it and that's it. It's not that I mind answering questions, but it's nice that he's not just relying on me to tell him everything about everything, especially when I feel like there's so much more for me to learn myself.

My knuckles relax a little. "I thought that could be related. I'm waiting to hear back from the universities I applied to. That's been sort of stressful, I guess."

"University of Toronto, McGill, and Queen's, right?"

"Right."

"All on the east."

"Yeah."

"Wherever you decide to go, it'll be a big move across the country. That can definitely be stressful to think about," he says. "How does your dad feel about you moving away for school?"

"We don't really talk about that kind of stuff."

"School?"

"Feelings."

The anger that I pushed down earlier this morning

threatens to rise back up, hot and biting and sudden. "He won't even talk to me about my condition," I say, folding my arms across my chest. "Or how I want to see a specialist. He's just so closed-minded about it. He keeps saying I'll grow out of it, as if he's the expert and I'm not the one who's constantly walking around, worried that I'll vanish at any given moment. I mean, speaking of stress, yeah, I guess I would consider that pretty stressful."

The words come rushing out, frustration banging on my chest like a drum. But as soon as I finish, something like shame grabs my anger and drags it back down, leaving me numb again. All I can see is Appa's face over his cereal bowl, pleading with me to understand. Even now, even here, I don't want to let him down. But why can't he see that I'm just asking him the same thing? To see where I'm coming from?

"Would it be helpful if we spoke with your father together about this?" Mr. Riaga asks. "Sometimes it can help to hear things from a third party. And I personally think it would be good for you to be connected with a specialist."

I can't help the lump that rises in my throat. I'm touched, again, and I feel guilty for thinking earlier that Mr. Riaga hasn't been very helpful. If anyone could convince Appa to consider taking me to a specialist, it would probably be the calming, personable, adult school counselor Mr. Riaga.

"That would be great," I say, my voice thick with almost-tears. I clear my throat. "Thank you."

"Okay." He nods. "Okay. How about I give him a call and ask him to come into a meeting?"

"Yeah, that sounds good." My phone buzzes inside my pocket and I say a quick sorry, pulling it out to silence it. I catch a glimpse of the screen.

Nikita:

Where are you? We're starting to set up for the auction!

Oh shoot. "Sorry, Mr. Riaga, but is it okay if I go now? I promised Nikita I'd help set up for the grad auction."

He waves me toward the door. "Go on. I'll keep you updated on our meeting. Good chat today!"

Mr. Riaga ends every meeting with "Good chat today!" even if the chat was just mediocre. Today, though, I agree. I feel more hopeful than I have all day.

"Thanks again," I say, smiling.

As I head out of his office and down the hall, I text Nikita that I'm on my way. My steps feel lighter. Some of the numbness is even starting to lift.

Maybe everything is going to be okay.

I turn the corner, about to pass by the woodwork classroom as the door swings open, narrowly missing smacking me right in the face.

"Sorry!" a student wearing goggles over his head and holding one end of what looks like a lopsided handmade table says. "Didn't see you there."

"It's okay. Nice table."

"Yeah? You like it?" He sighs. "Mr. Leon only gave us a C-plus, but I thought it was worth at least a B. He kept saying how we lost points because all the legs are different sizes, but isn't that what gives it character? I mean, fine, maybe a B-minus at the least—"

"Any day now, Matt, this thing isn't exactly made of feathers," the student holding the other end of the table grunts.

"Here, let me help," I say, moving to hold the door open for them.

As I pull the door open wider, the smell of sawdust fills my nose.

It's nothing I haven't smelled before. It's just sawdust, ordinary sawdust. I've walked by this room a hundred times, even took a woodworking elective last year, the woodsy smell dusting my palms, sticking to my clothes. It's never been anything but another scent. Not a trigger.

But this time, I can tell something's off right away.

It's quick. A moment, half a second, a breath at most, that my mind registers what's happening. Panic flares in my chest, but before I can do anything or so much as say a word, the door handle slips from my fingers, and I'm gone.

FILE: AIMEE ROH

Disappearance Number Seven

Date of incident: Tues 1/17

Details: Trigger scent, chalkboard eraser dust. Third period, Ms. Morris's math class, four minutes. Memory of drawing chalk art on the sidewalk (four years old). She was drawing a family portrait (Aimee, Dad, Mom).

Note to self: Talk to Ms. Morris about switching to a whiteboard.

Disappearance Number Eight

Date of incident: Mon 2/20

Details: Trigger scent, raspberry syrup on snow cones. After school, snow cone stall for grad fundraiser, one minute. Memory of spilling raspberry juice on herself (three years old) at the park and looking around for Mom, calling her name. Unsure where Mom was or if she appeared.

Note to self: How much are these kids even making from selling snow cones? Does the benefit outweigh the cost of putting this stall together?

Disappearance Number Nine

Date of incident: Wed 3/1

Details: Trigger scent, corn tea and cigarettes. She had tea in thermos and kids were smoking under the bleachers (look into this). During lunch with Nikita Lai-Sanders, gone for two minutes. Not ready to share about memory yet.

Note to self: Call Aimee's dad about specialist.

Four

Describe what it feels like to disappear in ten words or less.

It's something like this: déjà vu but you can't quite place it.

For the first few seconds, everything is sawdust. You don't know how loud a scent can be until it uproots you. After that, you realize the way it can ring in your ears, make your head throb, reverberate, grabbing you by the bones and shaking, not letting go.

One sense at a time. It's a piece of advice I picked up from the STWS forums. *Going back to a memory can be disorienting. Name where you are one sense at a time to ground yourself.*

What do you see? I take slow, deep breaths, trying to calm the panic I feel at suddenly arriving somewhere foreign. It's dim, though there's an orange light coming from my left. I let my eyes adjust to the dark and I realize I'm in the upstairs loft of a cabin and the light is coming from downstairs. There's not much up here. Just a dresser drawer, a twin-sized bed, and a little girl tucked under the covers, awake and thumbing through a Pokémon guidebook, squinting to read in the minimal light.

Me.

What do you smell? I know where I am. The panic ebbs a bit as recognition clicks in. It's Salt Spring Island, the summer I turned six. We rented a cabin by the lake for the weekend to celebrate. Me, Appa, my mom. It was our first and last vacation with all three of us. The cabin was freshly built and still smelled like sawdust. I was thrilled by the loft, wanted to sleep up there all by myself. The smell was strongest up here. I didn't care. I loved this smell.

And what do you feel?

This one is tricky. I run my fingers lightly over the loft railing, but like always when I touch objects in a memory, it feels like nothing. It's like someone has traced the shape of it with air and the outline is all I can feel. When I try to grasp anything more firmly—turning a doorknob, pressing a button, even placing a hand onto a burning stove—I go right through it like a ghost, feeling nothing. The only thing that stays solid the whole time is the ground I walk on, and even that feels strangely like stepping on firm air.

I can't touch things here and no one can see or hear or touch me either.

The smell's not so strong anymore as I adjust to my surroundings and my ears start opening up to the sounds around me. Not that there's much. Just the ever-so-quiet sound of flipping pages as Memory Me tries to read her Pokémon book without alerting anyone. I smile at that.

I don't remember much about this trip, to be honest, but I do remember that book. I carried it around with me everywhere, folding dog ears on all my favorite Pokémon.

As far as visiting old memories goes, this one's not so bad. It's cozy, even. Maybe I can sit next to Memory Me and look through the book together for the few minutes that I'm here.

What else do you hear?

The sound of a shower running, somewhere downstairs. I peer over the railing and then my breath catches.

Sitting on the couch, right below me, is my mom. She's staring absent-mindedly at the framed paintings of sailboats on the wall, her chin propped in her hand, elbow pressed into the cushion on her lap. Her hair is long and loose over her shoulders, thick and half curly like mine. I remember as a kid thinking that my mom would make the perfect ballerina figurine inside a music box because she was beautiful and good at being still. I remember she sat still a lot, staring into the air.

I'm so transfixed by her that I don't even realize the shower has stopped until Appa walks into the room, hair wet, a towel around his shoulders. He's wearing a T-shirt and sweatpants and, as always when I see him in my childhood memories, I'm taken aback by how much he's aged. He looks so young here.

"Aimee still sleeping?" Appa says to my mom in Korean.

"Mm," she replies.

"Maybe I'll go check on her. Make sure she's doing all right on her own."

He makes his way toward the loft stairs.

Memory Me freezes in her bed. She hurriedly stuffs the Pokémon book under the covers and closes her eyes. A rush of remembering runs through me. I remember exactly what I was thinking in that moment. That I had to try to be as still as my mom to convince Appa I was asleep this whole time.

But he never comes up, just like I remember. Back then, I was relieved that my mom said something to him just in time to call him back down. I didn't even register what she said. I was already pulling the Pokémon book back out of my covers.

Now, revisiting, I hear what I missed then.

"I don't think I can do this anymore."

Appa's feet pause on the steps. He turns around. "What do you mean?"

My mom keeps her eyes on the sailboats. "I can't stop thinking about going back. Starting fresh. I dream about it. When I'm awake and when I'm sleeping. It's like it calls to me."

"What calls to you?" Appa's voice is quiet. "Korea?"

"Everything."

My brow furrows. What is that supposed to mean? What is *everything*?

Appa walks back to the couch, kneels in front of my

mom so he's looking her in the eye. "Please don't talk about leaving again," he says.

Again? My frown deepens. When did she ever talk about leaving?

Ever since the day she walked out on us, Appa has said it was completely out of the blue, that she'd never once mentioned it. Even when I asked if he was sure, completely sure, that there was nothing he could think of, no clues that she left, he'd say, "No. There was nothing."

"She left without a word" became the blanket statement I used to tell the story, to Nikita, to Mr. Riaga. All we heard was that she was in Korea, so we knew she was safe. Appa said maybe she just needed some alone time, that she would come home one day.

She never did, but I always got the feeling that Appa never stopped waiting.

Is it because he knew the real reason why she left?

Why would he lie to me about that?

"You've already been disappearing so often lately," Appa says quietly. "Please don't talk about actually leaving for good."

"You know I can't help the disappearing," she says. "It's getting harder and harder to control."

"I know. But just think of the good life we've built here. Think of Aimee. It was all worth it for her, wasn't it?"

My mom says nothing.

What do you taste?

Confusion, like biting into a bitter melon without knowing what it is. It seeps onto my tongue and settles in my gut, twisting. I don't understand what's happening. My brain starts to feel fuzzy. Disappearing? Harder to control? What does that mean? The words feel at once familiar and foreign, like looking into a mirror expecting to see myself and seeing my mom instead. I can't wrap my head around it, not here.

How many minutes has it been? I fumble for my phone to check the time, forgetting that every time I disappear, the clock on my phone freezes to the time I vanished and doesn't start moving again until I'm back. It's stuck at 3:21 p.m.

This has definitely been longer than two minutes. Maybe even longer than my longest time, ten. I suddenly feel claustrophobic. How much more do I have to stay here?

I turn to Memory Me. If she sleeps, maybe the memory will end and I can go back. But she's not in bed anymore. I startle, realizing she's right beside me, peering through the railings at Appa and my mom.

And then my stomach sinks. Because I remember how the rest of this night went.

I remember tiptoeing out of bed, curious about what my parents were talking about. I remember sensing that something was off and sitting by the railing, as quiet as possible, watching over them to see what would happen. I remember sitting there for hours because the answer is, nothing happened. Eventually Appa got up to go to bed.

I told myself I'd sleep when my mom did, but she just sat there staring at those sailboats.

As a six-year-old, I didn't know what it meant that she could be so still for hours, staring at nothing. I just knew that night that I wanted to try staying awake with her, even if she didn't know it, just in case she might be lonely.

As a seventeen-year-old, I still don't know what it means. But unlike how I used to be, all I want is to get out of here as fast as possible because my head feels stuffy and my heart is pounding in my ears.

It's like it calls to me.

What calls to you?

Everything.

It's getting harder and harder to control.

What does it mean?

She sits still. Memory Me sits still, eventually lying down to rest her head on the Pokémon book.

And because I have nowhere to go but here, nothing to do but wait, I sit still too, curling my knees into my chest. Trying to breathe. Waiting.

Waiting.

Waiting.

TOPIC: *Any advice for what to do when you come back from a memory?*

ProbablyEatingKettleCorn: Hi, everyone, looking for some advice. I was recently diagnosed with STWS and am struggling with the disappearing episodes. I'm 42, never had an issue with this before, but it just started happening a few months ago. Needless to say, this is all new to me, and the thing I'm struggling with the most is returning to the present after visiting a memory. It's so disorienting, especially when it happens in front of other people. At least when you go back to the past, no one can see you lose your shit. Do you have any tips on how to deal with this? Thanks in advance.

IchirakuRamenGuy33: Hi, KettleCorn. I have something called "My Standard Procedure List of Returning from the Past." It's like a mental checklist I use to reorient myself because, like you said, it's a mind trip coming back. Feel free to tweak as necessary to fit your needs:

AND THEN JUST LIKE THAT. Cool, you're in the present again. Give yourself time to recognize that you're no longer in the memory by making note of your changed surroundings.

HOW LONG WAS I GONE FOR? Check the time to know how long you were gone. You've probably already noticed that you'll have to restart your phone to get the correct time when you're back (or your watch if you're a watch person, in which case you'll need to figure out the right time in order to reset your watch).

WHAT NOW? Pretty self-explanatory. After you've got the first two down, figure out what you're supposed to do next. Like the immediate next step (going back to sleep, continuing on with your job, leaving for that appointment you're now late for, whatever). Try not to think too far ahead so you don't get overwhelmed.

EVERYTHING WILL BE ALL RIGHT. Take a breath. Get your heart rate down. Remind yourself that you're safe and everything's going to be all right.

Five

AND THEN JUST LIKE THAT.

    I gasp.

Coming back always hits me like a shock of electricity, bright and sudden. One second, I'm trying to keep myself awake and sane by looking at Pokémon stats over Memory Me's shoulder, and then I blink and the cabin's gone, Charmander's gone, younger me is gone, and I'm alone in a dark, empty hallway, next to the woodworking classroom. Right back where I started.

I lean against the classroom door, trying to steady my shaky breath. Relief washes over me as I press a palm against my chest, heart racing.

I'm back. Finally. Finally.

The relief slowly ebbs into something more muted, my brain shifting into autopilot mode.

HOW LONG WAS I GONE FOR?

I fumble for my phone, which still says 3:21 p.m. I turn it off and on again, waiting for it to restart. The screen lights up with my background photo—a picture I took at H Mart of a pile of persimmons stacked precariously on top of each other—and the time.

12:13 a.m.

My mind goes still and silent. I knew I was gone for a long time, the longest I've ever been gone, but nine hours?

I missed the grad auction, I think.

And then, *Who set up the chairs?*

My phone screen floods with missed calls and messages, appearing all at once. Nikita. Nikita. Nikita again. And then a dozen in a row from Appa.

I never come home late, and if I do, Appa always knows about it. He wouldn't have called the cops to file a missing person report, would he?

WHAT NOW?

I swipe at the screen to call Appa back, lifting the phone to my ear as I walk down the hallway, slowly at first, and then I run. The phone rings. I race for the front entrance, but the doors are locked tight. I pull as hard as I can on the handle, as if that'll make a difference in opening a door that's locked from the inside and out. As if that'll really change anything.

The phone keeps ringing. I keep pulling.

And then the ringing stops and Appa's voice fills my ear. "Aimee?" he says, urgent and loud. "Where are you?"

"I'm okay. I'm at school." My voice comes out small. I clear my throat, not wanting him to worry even in a situation like this. "Can you come get me? You might need to call the janitor."

EVERYTHING WILL BE ALL RIGHT.

By the time Appa arrives with Karl, the janitor, it's past 1:00 a.m. Appa rushes to me, putting his hands on my shoulders and giving me a quick once-over. Once he's made sure that I'm as okay as I said I was, we both thank Karl profusely.

"You're the Time Syndrome girl, aren't you?" The janitor's cheek is marked with pillow creases. I'll have to bring him a coffee in the morning to make up for this. I nod and he sighs, scowling deep. "Next time, can you have your disappearances during school hours?"

My face flushes with embarrassment. "It's not like I can control it," I say under my breath.

"What's that?"

"I said it's not like I can control it," I repeat, louder. Usually, I would say nothing. I would just let it go. But I'm so damn tired and shaken that the words come out before I can stop them. "Do you think I wanted to be locked up in the school by myself in the middle of the night?"

Karl sighs again, shaking his head. "Teenagers. You all get more selfish by the year. You think your actions only affect yourselves, huh?"

"Am I supposed to be thinking of anyone other than myself right now?" I say in disbelief. "I was just—"

"Aimee, that's enough." Appa steps in, cutting me off. He bows his head to Karl. "We're sorry for waking you up and dragging you into this. Thank you very much again for helping."

Karl waves us off with a grumpy, "All right, all right, get out of here then. My night's been interrupted enough." Appa puts a hand on my shoulder and steers me away. I'm so stunned that I let him. I can feel Karl watching us as we head for our car, eyes trailing me with disdain.

The ride home is quiet. Appa's shoulders are tense as he drives, but he doesn't say anything. I sit there, hands clenched on my knees. *Why didn't you defend me in front of Karl?* I want to say. *Why didn't you believe me when I said this was a problem?* But I don't want to be the first to speak. I want him to say something, to acknowledge what happened tonight, to acknowledge this, all of this. But even now, he won't talk to me.

Frustration rises in my chest, clashing against my desire to keep the peace, to not cause him any more stress than I already have.

I break the silence first. "I told you the disappearing was a problem."

I want it to sound as angry as I feel. If he had just believed me, if he had just given me help when I asked for it, maybe this wouldn't have happened. But right now, I'm more exhausted than I am mad, and it comes out as more of a half-hearted mutter.

He's quiet for a moment, not taking his eyes off the road, and then he says, "As long as you're okay now, everything will be all right."

I turn my face away and close my eyes.

Nikita:

Hey you. Hope you're having a good R&R day.

Nikita:

Lmk if you need anything.

Nikita:

I can skip class to come over or talk on the phone any time, just say the WORD!

I lie in bed and stare at my phone as Nikita's texts pop up. I messaged her last night when I got home to let her know that I was safe and alive, and then again this morning to say I was taking a sick day. The I'm-Sorry Coffee for Karl will have to wait. *Are you ok?* Nikita asked at my morning text. *Yes*, I wrote back, *totally fine. Just tired from yesterday's . . .*

Yesterday's what? Yesterday's episode? Yesterday's blip in time? Yesterday's completely perplexing encounter with my mom from the past?

Her words play in a loop in my head. *You know I can't help the disappearing. It's getting harder and harder to control.* I haven't been able to shake it. Could that mean what I think it means?

I ended up backspacing and sending it as: *just tired from*

yesterday. That was at 7:00 a.m.

It's noon now. I appreciate Nikita checking in again, but I can't find the energy to reply this time. I know she's worried and probably more than a little curious about what happened exactly, but that's the thing. I can't even answer that question for myself.

I just want to stay in bed all day. Do nothing but think. Or not think. Even better. Just drift. It's not unusual for me to feel out of it after a memory trip, but I can't remember it ever feeling this bad. This foggy and confusing. I want to ignore it all, and the whole world with it.

But then my stomach grumbles and I finally haul myself out of bed to dig around the kitchen for food. There's a Post-it note on the fridge written in Korean: *Heat up the kimchi jjigae on the stove to eat. There's rice in the rice cooker.*

Appa's writing is neat and precise, like a font. I pop open the rice cooker lid and let the steam billow into my face. I heard him this morning clattering around the kitchen in his usual routine. There was an extended stretch of silence, like maybe he was waiting for me to come out of my room and pour my bowl of cereal, just the same as always. Or maybe he was quietly reading the news, lost in his own world, just the same as always. Either way, I heard him move again shortly after that, the sound of dishes and running water, and then the click of the door locking as he left for work. I guess he somehow squeezed in time to make fresh rice before leaving.

I heat up the kimchi jjigae. Somewhere under the numb haze in my mind, I register gratitude to Appa for taking the time to prepare this. And then under that, anger, simmering hot and red like the stew on the stove. He never asked where I went yesterday. I was gone for nine hours, and he didn't even care what I was doing or who I was seeing. Hell, he seemed to care more about disrupting Karl than about what happened to me.

Please don't talk about leaving again.

His words to my mom from yesterday's memory burn in my thoughts. Did he know? Did he know she was going to leave? And if he did, why would he tell me that she left without a word or a single sign? Has he been lying to me all these years?

I sit down at the table with the jjigae and a bowl of rice and log on to the STWS forums on my phone. I've been on this forum for years, but I've never made a single post myself. I'm basically a professional lurker by now. Except for that one time when I did participate in something from the forums. The STWS meetup.

Meetups are organized in various cities around the world for people with STWS to connect with each other in person. There have been a few in Vancouver, and last year, I finally convinced Appa to let me go to one. He'd been wary about me meeting a group of strangers from the internet, but after my disappearance at the art show, I was feeling desperate to connect with other people like me. He finally gave in, on the condition that he go with me.

The meetup was at a Starbucks. I walked in, scanning the room, searching for a group of people who I might feel an immediate, unspoken kindred connection with. A woman from a table of five spotted me looking around and tentatively waved me over.

"Are you here for the STWS meetup?" she asked.

I said I was. Appa and I introduced ourselves and so did the others. They were all older than me, a range of university students and working adults, and I was hyper-aware of the fact that I was sixteen and here with my dad. I felt awkward. No, not just me. The whole vibe felt a bit awkward. I wondered if it was everyone's first time here.

Hassan, who introduced himself as a third year at Langara College, cleared his throat. "I was just telling everyone before you got here that this is my cousin Cole." He gestured to the person next to him wearing a backward baseball cap and a big toothy grin. "He, um, doesn't have STWS, but he asked if it was okay for him to sit in on our meetup. He's making a documentary about STWS for his film class."

"Oh," I said in surprise. "Um . . ."

"This isn't being filmed, is it?" Appa asked, frowning.

"No, no, I'm just observing and taking some notes," Cole said cheerfully. "I'm a current film major, future film director, and I think STWS is such an important topic that isn't talked about enough. So I thought, what better topic for my documentary project than this? You won't be mentioned in the film or anything, I'm just here to gather research. Though if you *are* comfortable with me interviewing you, we can talk about that after. Everyone here already gave me their consent, but if you're not okay with it . . ."

An extended silence lingered in the air. Appa narrowed his eyes at Cole and leaned over to me, muttering under his breath, "Galkka?"

Part of me wanted to say yes, let's go. This wasn't at all how I'd pictured my first meetup and I felt more than a little uncomfortable having to watch what I said in front of a current film major, future film director. But I just got here and it took so much convincing to even get this far.

"It's fine," I said. "As long as I'm not going to be quoted in the documentary or anything?"

"Only with your consent if there's anything that I think is quote-worthy," Cole said, beaming. "And of course, I won't write down anything anyone wants me to avoid. So go ahead, just pretend I'm not here."

He motioned with his hands for us to carry on, picking up his notebook and pen.

"Um, so, how is everyone doing?" Lora, the woman who first waved me over, asked.

The conversation, stilted at first, slowly rolled along until the awkwardness began to lift. One of the older adults, Dylan, broke the ice by sharing about how their trigger sense is touch, specifically whenever they touch anything cold, which makes the winters quite difficult. Another person, Zaina, shared how she disappeared any time she saw shooting stars, real or otherwise. It was fascinating, hearing about their STWS, so similar to but different from mine. *This*. This was what I stayed for. I took a deep breath and had opened my mouth to share about my sense when Cole raised his pen in the air.

"Sorry to interrupt," he said, looking not at all sorry to interrupt. "But I just have to ask because I'm so curious . . . Hassan told me that people with STWS have the possibility of getting stuck in a time loop. Has that ever happened to any of you?"

Time loops? As far as I knew, time loops were pure speculation, something like a myth that people liked to whisper about on the forums every now and then. It was the idea that a person could get stuck in a memory they visited, becoming trapped in a never-ending loop without ever returning to the present. Honestly, just thinking about it gave me goose bumps. I tried to avoid those threads as much as possible.

Hassan looked mortified. "I told you it was just a theory."

"But what about the story of Benji Grey-Diaz?" Cole said, dropping his voice to a loud whisper when he said the name. "You know, the American snowboarder with STWS who went missing right before his Olympic debut?"

Everyone around the table stiffened. Of course we'd all heard of Benji Grey-Diaz. Not only is he one of the few public figures with STWS that we know of, but his mysterious disappearance last winter was broadcasted on every news outlet, blaring in the headlines because of how strange it was. He vanished without a trace the night before his half-pipe run, and people in the forums started speculating that maybe he disappeared into a time loop. The rumor spread to the news and for a while it felt like everyone was talking about it, but without any evidence to back it up, the rumor fizzled as quickly as it had started. Benji Grey-Diaz is still missing today.

"Anything could have happened to him," Lora said. "We don't know for sure it was a time loop. Besides, like Hassan said, the whole thing is just a theory. To answer your earlier question, it's never happened to me before." The others nodded in agreement.

"Okay, but let's say the theory is real," Cole pressed. "What do you think would cause someone to get stuck in a time loop? And could they ever get out of one? How do you think it would feel?"

"I mean, it would probably feel terrifying," Zaina said flatly. "That sounds like the stuff of nightmares, no? Whatever happened to Benji Grey-Diaz, I'm sure all of us hope that it has nothing to do with STWS."

"Tell me more," Cole said, pen poised.

"Uh, I don't really have more to say."

Hassan looked like he was having some major regrets about bringing Cole to this meeting. "Please, let this go.

We were in the middle of a conversation."

"Why?" Cole asked. "Aren't you all curious about it too? It's, like, such a cool part of your condition! I think people would be super interested in learning about this in my documentary."

Dylan raised an eyebrow, folding their arms across their chest. "It's cool to disappear from your life and be trapped somewhere where no one can find you?"

"Uh, well, no, that's not what I meant," Cole said, backtracking. "I just want to help raise awareness about what you all go through, and I thought time loops could be a good, previously unexplored angle to do that. It's a great hook for drawing people in."

"I'm so sorry," Hassan mouthed to the rest of the table. I felt bad for him. It wasn't Hassan's fault that his cousin couldn't read the room. Clearly none of us wanted to talk about this with someone who was just using us as entertainment fodder for his school project, but Cole either didn't realize how insensitive he was being or didn't care.

Either way, it was hard to revive the conversation after that and it wasn't long until the meetup ended with Cole passing out his email on slips of paper, telling us to get in touch if we wanted to be interviewed for his project. Appa took the paper on my behalf and threw it in the garbage can on our way out.

I haven't gone back to a meetup since. As much as I liked the others I met there, I decided that it was safer to just explore what I wanted to know online. Meeting people in person came with too much unpredictable territory.

I eat a spoonful of rice and jjigae, fingers still poised over my phone. I think again of last night's memory with my mom and then type into the forum search engine: *STWS hereditary?*

A thread pops up with the title: *Anyone else have family members with the same condition?* I scroll through the replies.

stargazinginhelsinki01: *I definitely think it's hereditary. My dad has it and so did his dad.*

1234margarine: *No. There's zero history of STWS in my family. I'm the first one, and I don't even think they believe I really have it. I swear, they think I'm just hiding in a broom closet for attention whenever I disappear.*

LordGnomeAndMinions: *Same as margarine. Just me in my family.*

ro_chang_87: *I thought I was the only one in my family, but I found out that my late aunt had it too, I just never knew. Shame. It would have been nice to have someone close to me to talk to about it.*

I linger on that last comment. *I just never knew.* The haze in my mind begins to lift—no, not lift. It gets swallowed, devoured, by a desperate curiosity rising to take its place.

Did my mom have STWS too?

FROM THE PAGES OF AIMEE'S JOURNAL

THINGS I KNOW

- I have Sensory Time Warp Syndrome.
- My trigger is scent. The disappearances are random, but they are happening more and more often.
- My mom also said she "had a hard time controlling her disappearances" (paraphrased).

THINGS I DON'T KNOW

- Why my disappearances are increasing.
- How to stop them from increasing.
- What my mom meant by what she said.
- If her disappearances were related to STWS or something else.
- Why Appa would say her leaving us was unexpected when he seemed to have a pretty good idea of it before it happened.
- Why there are so many more things that I don't know than I do know.

Six

I can't believe I'm doing this, but desperate times call for desperate measures. I've been scrolling through the forums like mad with my journal by my side, reading, searching, for what exactly I'm not sure. I've just been writing down all my questions and thoughts and whatever tidbits have been coming up online. *Did my mom have STWS? Why do I keep seeing her in my memories? Are my disappearances trying to tell me something?* It's the feeling when you have so many questions overlapping with each other that you don't even know what answer you're looking for. You just know that you're looking. But the forums only have so much, and I need something more.

I sit on the living room couch with my laptop and type in a new Google search: *Cole, STWS documentary.*

The first link that pops up is his documentary, a twenty-minute video on YouTube titled "The Unseen Reality of Sensory Time Warp Syndrome."

My cursor hovers over the link. Oh god. Do I really want to subject myself to this? I hesitate and then I click.

The documentary opens with a string of clips from various

time travel movies, playing first at regular speed and then faster and faster and faster and then cutting abruptly to a black screen.

"Time travel," a voice that I recognize as Cole's says. "We know what it looks like in fiction. But what does it look like in reality?"

Music from *The X-Files* starts to play as Cole narrates over random B-roll footage of people walking down the street. "Sensory Time Warp Syndrome. A condition where people travel back in time to their memories when triggered by one of the five senses: sight, sound, smell, taste, and touch. There, they must resist the urge to alter the past and change the course of history for all mankind. So how do they do it? How does it feel to be a real-life time traveler?"

I roll my eyes. Okay. This isn't even accurate. I hope he got a terrible grade. I don't know why I entertained the idea of watching this. Clearly, I'm not going to learn anything new here.

Just as I'm about to close the video, Hassan's face appears on the screen. He's sitting at a kitchen table, mini microphone clipped to the collar of his plaid shirt, face angled slightly away from the camera like he's speaking to an interviewer behind the lens. I guess Cole managed to get at least one person to interview for his documentary. His cousin. I leave the video on.

"We can't actually change the past," Hassan says with a slight laugh. "We can only see it unfold exactly the way it did when it happened and then we come back to the present. It's not as interesting as you put it."

"What sends you back to the past?" Cole's voice asks off-screen.

"My trigger sense is sound. So when I hear certain things that remind me of a memory, I get sent back there for a brief moment in time. The sound of a train, for example, or the sound of thunder."

"Can you share what memories you go back to?"

Hassan smiles with his lips tightly closed. "They're just personal memories. Probably boring for you to know."

"Okay, that's fine. What would you say is the hardest part of time traveling?"

"The hardest part?" Hassan pauses for a moment. "I suppose for me, the hardest part would be going back to memories I don't necessarily want to revisit. There's nothing you can do about it, you just have to wait for it to play out, and that can be challenging. But I've found that sometimes, there are reasons why I visit memories that are more difficult in nature. Sometimes it's a sign that there are things from the past I haven't resolved or that I need to find closure in. I mean, that might just be me reading into things that aren't there, but personally, I've found this to be true with certain memories. Not all of them, but some."

"Fascinating," Cole says. "Now what can you tell me about time loops?"

Hassan sighs. "Next question?"

The screen cuts to stock footage of someone in a white lab coat frantically writing on a chalkboard with the *X-Files* music playing again. "Time loops," Cole's voiceover says. "A concept so mythical, so terrifying, that even those with STWS don't know how to describe it . . ."

I'm hoping for more interviews, but the rest of the video is just more of Cole's over-the-top narration. I turn it off and close my laptop.

I lean my head back against the couch and stare up at the ceiling. Cole's documentary and future as a director was about as enlightening as I thought it would be—that is to say, not at all—but there was a piece of it that struck me. Hassan, the only real part of that video.

I open my journal and write: *Sometimes it's a sign that there are things from the past I haven't resolved or that I need to find closure in . . . Not all of them, but some.*

Closure.

I rifle through my journal. Every time I have a disappearance, I make note of it here. I've never seen a distinct pattern to my memories before, but lately, there's clearly been a common thread. I don't need a specialist to tell me that. My own writing stares back at me, glaring with the evidence.

Disappearance Number Six. Grapefruit and musk, my mom at the library.

Disappearance Number Seven. Chalk dust, drawing family portrait on the sidewalk.

Disappearance Number Eight. Raspberry syrup, looking for my mom after the juice box spill.

Disappearance Number Nine. Corn tea and cigarettes, seeing Appa cry for the first time.

And of course, *Disappearance Number Ten. Sawdust, Salt Spring Island.*

Before that, the last memory my mom was the center of was Disappearance Number Two, when the scent of maple syrup took me back to a time when Appa tried making pancakes but burned them all. My mom said it was a waste to throw them out, so she scraped off the burnt layer and used double the amount of syrup to mask the charred taste. It was terrible, but she said the sweetness reminded her of the dalgona she used to eat as a kid—flat circle-shaped candy with a shape in the middle that you try to pop out without breaking—and she finished the whole thing. I didn't even remember that memory until I returned to it. So why is she coming up so much now?

Is my subconscious trying to tell me something? That I need to find some kind of closure with her if I want to stop disappearing so much? Hassan's voice plays in my head. *Sometimes it's a sign.* Is this a sign? From God or the universe or my own brain telling me that there's truth to be uncovered, and it won't let me rest until I find it?

"This is absurd," I say to nobody.

But what if? What if it's not? What if it *is* a sign and finding the answers to all my questions about my mom will mean I vanish less? I could breathe a little easier. Have all my firsts. Dates and dances and driver's licenses. Show my art without fear.

I could really live my life.

My mom's face comes back to me, drawn and distant, sitting in the Salt Spring Island cabin. If she does have STWS too, she would know exactly how I feel. I would know how she feels. Maybe she would never have left if she knew that in a few years' time, I would also have STWS. If she stayed, we could have been there for each other through all of this. If we meet again now, maybe we still can be.

There's the sound of jingling keys and the front door unlocks. I look up to see Appa walk in, carrying a box of pizza. I can't believe he's already home from work. How long have I been sitting here like this?

"Hey, Appa," I say, shoving my laptop and journal under a couch cushion. I put on a smile.

"Hey." He holds up the box. "I got pizza."

"Great, I'm starving," I say brightly.

I don't know why I feel guilty, like he's caught me doing something I'm not supposed to. I guess I always feel that way when I think about my mom. It's hard to remember now, but before she left, Appa and I could talk about anything. But then she was gone and there was something we couldn't talk about anymore. I learned early on that he would avoid any mention of her and that she was a topic I should best avoid too. Then, shortly after that, there was my STWS diagnosis. Another topic he didn't want to entertain. Everything we couldn't talk about slowly stacked up between us until there were so many things we couldn't say, it got easier to simply say nothing at all.

"Aimee?"

I blink. Appa's already at the kitchen table, opening the box of pizza. I get up to join him.

It's half Hawaiian, half True Canadian with jalapeño ranch dipping sauce. My favorite pizza order. I wonder if he'll ask me how my day was, how I'm feeling about the disappearance yesterday, if I want to talk about the memory.

But he doesn't, so we eat in silence.

I'm searching for the words, trying to figure out how to ask him about my mom in a way that might make him open to talking about her, when he says, "Your school counselor called me today."

I nearly drop my pizza slice. "Mr. Riaga?"

"Yeah."

My heart lifts. Bless Mr. Riaga, coming through on his promise to call Appa about me seeing a specialist. This couldn't have come at a better time. "What did he say?"

"Nothing much. He was just worried about you, but I told him you're doing much better." Appa surveys my face. "And it seems to be true. You're more cheerful today."

I blink. I don't know what to say. "I . . . Um . . . He didn't mention anything about a meeting? Or about me seeing a therapist?"

"Oh. He did, but I told him it's not necessary. We're taking care of it."

"Are we taking care of it?" I ask, bewildered. *Don't rock the boat, Aimee*, a voice in the back of my head says. *Don't make this uncomfortable.* But I can't help it. I need to know. "How exactly are we taking care of it?"

"Well, you took the day off school and you're feeling better, right?" Appa says. "All you needed was some rest."

I stare at him. I can't believe he thinks it's so simple. "Appa, I was missing for nine hours yesterday."

"But you're back now and everything's fine. Besides, that was a one-time thing. It'll never happen again."

"How can you guarantee that?" I cry, my voice rising.

He stares at me, surprise in his eyes at me speaking back so loudly. And then the surprise shifts into something more familiar, a silent entreaty, hanging in the air between us. *Let this go. Let's just eat our dinner in peace.* "It's like we talked about yesterday morning. You'll have to try harder not to do that anymore. You're a smart, resourceful girl. I know you can do it. It's a matter of practice, okay? Don't give up."

He smiles, turning back to his pizza, and the way he does it, eyes going distant, withdrawing again to that place I can't follow, it makes me suddenly realize. No matter what I say, how much I vanish, or who tries to convince him, Appa won't see what he doesn't want to see. I keep waiting for him to come around, but he never will. He'll never listen, never be on my side the way I need him to be, never understand that this thing I'm supposed to just willpower my way through doesn't work like that.

I slowly drop my pizza on my plate and excuse myself from the table.

I get it now, I think as I go to my room and close the door, leaning against it.

I'm really alone.

Seven

"**P**ancakes?"

Nikita looks up from her menu with a grin, already flagging down our server at IHOP like she knows my answer before I even say it. Which, of course, she does. As soon as she called me this morning and asked me out to breakfast, I knew we would be sharing our usual full stack of buttermilk pancakes with a side of hash browns. I also knew she was trying to cheer me up. After all, pancakes are a healing food.

"Please," I say, closing my own menu. "And don't forget the—"

"Hash browns and a couple sharing plates. Of course. Who do you take me for?"

It's a Saturday and we just managed to squeeze into a corner booth before it got too busy. Nikita orders for us and then turns to me, her grin becoming a bit more tentative.

"How was your R and R yesterday?" she asks. "The morning drive wasn't the same without you."

"Oh, you know. I rested. I recovered. A classic R and R," I say, keeping my voice light. More like the exact opposite of a classic R & R, but I don't want to burden Nikita with the details of yesterday's spiral. "What'd I miss at school? Tell me all about the auction. I can't believe I missed it! Sorry again."

Nikita stares at me. "I wish you wouldn't do that."

"Do what?"

"I don't know. That." She waves a hand in my general direction. "That deflecting thing you do."

"I don't deflect."

"Ma'am, please. You are clearly FINE. And I mean that in all caps. Come on, talk to me."

I look down at the table, fiddling with the lids of the syrup containers. I like the classic maple syrup. Nikita always goes for the blueberry or strawberry. She thinks I'm Falling Into Never-ending Emptiness. And maybe I was, yesterday. After pizza dinner with Appa, I went into my room and pored over all the notes I took in my journal, every little thing I'd made note of from the rabbit hole I'd gone down. *Closure. Resolve. My mom is the common thread. Appa will never come around.* Eventually, I fell asleep with my face against the page, a heavy, dense, dreamless sleep that left me with a neck cramp in the morning.

Today, though. Today I feel better. I don't feel like I'm falling. Or at least, I can distract myself from the fact that I am. A toddler at the table next to us sticks his face into the whipped cream mountain on his waffle, his mother too frazzled to catch him in time. The bell over the front door keeps jingling as people walk in, the servers weaving through the tables with plates of bacon and eggs and French toast. The carpet is ugly, but that's what makes this place what it is. I'm just part of this, all of this, but if I talk to Nikita about what I'm actually feeling, I won't belong here anymore. Instead, I'll belong to the falling and it will overtake me.

It's easier just to pretend that everything is really okay. But the way Nikita's looking at me, I know she won't let me off the hook that easy. I hesitate, unsure where to start, and then I say, "The memory I went back to on Thursday night? It was from my childhood, where I overheard my parents talking. I didn't totally understand what they were saying, but my mom said something about how she's been disappearing a lot and it's been getting harder to control."

I leave out the part about Appa maybe knowing why she left and lying to me about it. For some reason, I feel protective of the fact. As mad as I am at him that this might be true, I don't want to make him look bad in front of Nikita.

"Anyway. I'm wondering if maybe she also had STWS like me and I just never knew about it?" I laugh a little, trying to brush it off. "It was such a small detail, I know, but it kind of stuck with me. And it's gotten me to think more about my mom in general. Why she left, what parts of the story I'm missing. I've been noticing that she's been showing up in my memories a lot lately."

Nikita's eyes grow wide and thoughtful. "That doesn't

sound like a small detail at all," she says. "It sounds like the opposite of small."

"Really?"

"Of course!"

"I mean, I guess it *could* be a big deal, huh?" I didn't want to weigh Nikita down with all my heavy thoughts, especially if I was making a big deal out of nothing, but hearing her say that unlodges something in me and the words come tumbling out before I can stop them. "Like what if, right? There's so much I don't know about her, but maybe this huge part of my life is something that we had in common. Maybe I keep seeing her in my memories these days because deep down in my subconscious I know that there's more I need to discover about her, something important, something that'll finally give me peace when I think about her instead of all these questions." I pause, pressing my lips together. "Not that there's anything I can do about it. She's not here, so. It doesn't change much."

"Isn't there any way you can contact her?" Nikita asks. Her tone is cautious. We don't talk about my mom very often, and I can tell she's choosing her words carefully, trying not to scare me off from this conversation. I realize belatedly that I didn't even tell Nikita that all my recent memories have been of my mom until now.

I shake my head. "All we know is that she's back in Korea, but we have no way of getting in touch with her."

Are you sure? a voice in my head nudges. If Appa knew

why she left, maybe he also knows where she is now. Maybe I'm the only one who doesn't know. I can add that to the list of Things I Don't Know in my journal.

"There's always a way," Nikita says confidently. "Would you want to talk to her if you could?"

I think for a moment. Would I? Yes. I would. I have complicated feelings about my mom, a woman who is now more of a fuzzy gap in my memory than a real person in my life. She left when I was so young that it's hard to remember who she was to me. I don't know what it would feel like to see her again. But *what if*? What if in some strange way, my memories are leading me to her? To seeking closure? And what if, a tinier hope in my heart says, she's the person in the world who would understand me more than anyone? More than even my friends and more, especially, than Appa?

I nod.

"Then go to Korea! Find her!" Nikita says, her voice rising with enthusiasm.

"Sorry to break it to you, Nik, but I think you're making it sound way easier than it is," I say.

"I'm telling you, there are ways. What about asking your dad for a list of contacts from their old friends in Korea? Or family members? You told me that you have family in Korea, right? Someone out there must know something about your mom and where she is now. And don't forget who you're talking to."

"Self-appointed member at large of the debate team?"

"No. Self-appointed social media detective."

"You mean creeper."

"Detective. Though I will accept 'investigator' as an acceptable second." Nikita straightens up. "I can help you. If you're able to find some information on the ground, I'll assist you online. And hey, maybe if you go to Korea you can even meet that cute tattoo boy again!"

"Cute tattoo boy . . . ?" It takes me a second to register that she's talking about my first crush, the one I visited in my memory about the hoddeok stall. I pick up a butter packet and throw it at her. "I knew I should have never told you about that! I was seven!"

"Yeah, and have you ever shown interest in anyone since?" Nikita says, dodging the butter. "Not that you need to or anything. But maybe you're soul mates. If you go to Korea, you can see him again."

"He doesn't even live there. He was just visiting for the summer."

"Soul mates always find a way."

Before I can respond, our server swoops in with our pancakes and hash browns. We push our water glasses out of the way to make room. Could I really go to Korea like Nikita is suggesting? To her, *impossible* is just a word, but I highly doubt Appa would willingly dole out contact info to help me find my mom, even if he had it. But then again, I do have an aunt in Korea who knew her. Gomo, Appa's older sister. Would she be willing to help?

No. This is ridiculous.

"I can't just go to Korea," I say.

"Why not?" Nikita asks as she divides the pancakes onto our shared plates. She reaches for the strawberry syrup, then changes her mind and grabs the blueberry. "It's spring break in a week. You'll have two whole weeks off school to do whatever you want."

"My dad would never agree to it."

"What does it hurt to ask?"

She takes a bite of her blueberry-syrup-doused pancakes and then reaches for the strawberry to add that too. I pick up my knife and rest it against the pancake without cutting it.

"What if she doesn't want to be found?" I ask quietly. "She left for a reason."

At this, Nikita puts down her fork and looks me in the eye, holding my gaze. "That might be true. But I've known you for a long time, Aimee, and these days . . . you've been different."

"What do you mean?"

"You're still Aimee Roh. But lately, I don't know, you just seem exhausted. It's like there's this huge weight on your shoulders that you're constantly carrying around. You don't say it, but I can see it. I think it could be good for you to do something just for yourself. I don't know if your mom wants to be found, but you can cross that bridge after you actually find her, right? One step at a time."

I didn't know Nikita thought I looked exhausted. Am

I exhausted? Maybe I am. Her words spark something in me, something stirring and true.

One step at a time. Weirdly, it makes sense. The thought of doing something more than just sitting in my room looking for answers on the internet is alluring, especially now knowing that Appa will never come around and give me the help I need. I can take this into my own hands. I can help myself.

"I can't believe you're seriously talking me into this," I say.

She grins. "Remember who you're talking to."

"Self-appointed social media creeper?"

"Detective. And no." She straightens up proudly, picking up her fork again. "Self-appointed member at large of the debate team."

Appa has Sundays off from the auto shop. He usually goes grocery shopping at H Mart and today, I volunteer to go with him. He looks surprised. Pizza dinner ended on an awkward note and we haven't talked much since then. But he doesn't protest. Just nods and gets in the car.

Nikita may have convinced me to consider the Korea idea, but convincing Appa? A whole other story, and I'm on my own for this one. I spent all night thinking about how I might bring it up. I wonder when talking to Appa always started requiring a night of planning in advance.

We stroll through H Mart, Appa pushing the grocery cart. I stop every so often to take a photo on my phone. I love taking pictures at grocery stores. There are so many colors and shapes and small, striking moments disguised in the mundane. I pause to take a photo of an H Mart employee stacking Korean sweet potatoes on top of each other. An idea comes to me.

"Hey, Appa, didn't my mom used to like those goguma a lot?" I ask.

It's a stab in the dark. I don't actually remember what food she particularly liked or disliked, but it's been ages since I've brought up my mom directly to Appa and I want to test the waters. Maybe he'll be more open to it now than I remember him being in the past, and I can segue into the truth about why I want to go to Korea. Not the whole STWS and finding closure to stop disappearing part, which I'm pretty sure he won't be into. But the curious about my mom part. A partial truth.

Appa stiffens, glancing sideways at the employee stacking potatoes.

"Not particularly," he says. He rolls the grocery cart along.

"Well then, what did she like?" I ask, jogging to keep up.

He doesn't reply. "I need pa," he says instead.

Okay. Going the truthful mom route isn't going to work. How does Nikita make persuasion look so easy? Different tactic.

"I was thinking," I say as Appa sifts through the green onions. "Spring break is coming up. Maybe it would be good for us to go on a vacation."

"A vacation?"

"Yeah."

"Where? Vancouver Island?"

"Actually, I was thinking somewhere farther away. Like Korea."

He stills. "Korea? Gapjagi wae?"

"It's not so out of the blue. We haven't gone in a long time and I was just thinking it would be nice. You know, before I go off to university."

He gets that look in his eyes. The faraway one. I'm worried I've broken him with all my words. I know I've gone way past my limit, but I don't know how to be succinct about this.

Snapshot: Appa grows roots next to the green onions. He becomes one of them, at home under the fluorescent lights and the sound of grocery cart wheels rattling against the floor. He is no longer Appa but just pa.

"Excuse me," a lady says, reaching past him for the green onions.

He blinks, returning to me, and steps out of the way. "I don't think so, Aimee."

"But why not? I have some money saved up from my summer job helping out at Nikita's mom's catering company. I can help cover the trip."

"I can't take that much time off," he says.

I hesitate. "I mean, I could go. By myself."

Appa and I may not talk all the time, but I can't remember a day when I haven't seen him. This would be the longest we've ever been apart. He stares at me.

"Andwae."

Just that one word. No.

"It'll be good for me to get a change of scenery," I try, suddenly desperate. It was a long shot, a wild plan, something I never would have thought of if Nikita hadn't planted the seed in my head. I knew Appa would never be on board. But now that I've started talking about it, I realize how badly I want this, no, how badly I *need* this, more than I was allowing myself to admit. "You know, with how much I've been disappearing lately, the fresh air would be helpful."

"You're too young to go by yourself," he says. He looks like he wants to say more, but he simply shrugs. "I'll see if I can take a couple days off and we can go to Victoria instead. Okay?"

He strolls ahead of me, pushing the cart.

He forgets to get green onions.

I can't go on like this.

The thought follows me as we leave H Mart, drive home, and turn the key to our apartment door. I put away the groceries in the kitchen, moving on autopilot.

Snapshot of me on the outside: dutifully tucking away the lettuce in the vegetable drawer, making sure it doesn't get crushed by the zucchinis, closing the refrigerator door and turning off the lights like I've just put them all to bed.

Snapshot of me on the inside: an explosion in a silent movie that shakes the screen but makes no sound. I feel nothing. I feel everything. Can a person suffocate in their own skin?

I can't go on like this.

"I'm going to take a shower," Appa says.

"Okay," I reply, standing at the counter arranging the garlic.

We could do this forever. And now I know, we will do this forever, because Appa won't change and I don't know how to make him.

But forever is such a long time to never have any firsts.

I stare at the garlic.

I can't go on like this.

I don't know if it's desperation or rebellion that comes over me, but in that moment, something snaps. I leave the garlic on the counter and start pulling out the kitchen drawers until I find it. There, Appa's extra credit card. It's specifically there for me to use in the event of an emergency and I am officially declaring this one.

The shower is running as I hurriedly walk past the bathroom and into my room, credit card gripped tight in my hand. I open my laptop and look up round-trip tickets from Vancouver to Korea. I will help myself. I will find my closure.

Fifteen minutes later, I've booked my tickets, sent a text to Gomo, and e-transferred part of the flight amount to Appa to pay off the bill. I send as much as I can with the savings from my summer job, but I don't have enough right now to cover everything, so I include how much I still owe him in the e-transfer notes.

I put the credit card back in the kitchen drawer. And then I sit and wait, hands knotted together, until the shower stops running.

Appa comes out a moment later, drying his hair with a towel and staring at his phone. "Why did you e-transfer me so much money?" he asks, looking up at me in confusion.

Deep breath. "Because," I say, "I'm going to Korea."

He stares. "What?"

"I'm sorry, Appa. I know you said no, but I really, really need this." I don't know how to explain this to him without bringing up all the topics he refuses to talk about, so I just say, "I need a break. I used the emergency credit card to book my flight. I promise I'll pay you back for the rest of the ticket as soon as I can."

"You did what?" He looks stunned, like he can't even wrap his mind around the fact that I went against his word. Honestly, neither can I. My heart is racing from adrenaline. And then he looks angry. "Aimee, I told you *no*. You're too young to go on your own. I can't believe you did this! We're returning these tickets right—"

His phone rings. He stares down at the screen and then

back up at me, his voice flat when he speaks. "Why is Gomo calling me right now?"

I say nothing.

He answers. "Hello?"

"Hyunwoo!" Gomo's voice chirps through the phone. "I just saw Aimee's message! Why didn't you tell me that she's coming to Korea? This is so wonderful! She'll be staying with me, of course. Are you coming too?"

He gives me a sharp look that says *You stay right there*, and then he leaves the kitchen, talking into the phone. "Hi, Nuna. About that . . ."

His bedroom door closes, and I can't hear any more. I let out a slow exhale, hands still clasped together on top of the table. The wait is excruciating. Please let this work out. Please let there be a way.

When he finally comes out of his room, his face is strained and almost shell-shocked. He looks like he's aged five years in the span of that one phone call. He stands still for a second, staring at me like he's not sure whether he should yell or simply throw me out of the house. Finally, he says, "Send me your itinerary."

I sit up straight. "My itinerary?"

"Your aunt insists that you come stay with her. She wouldn't take no for an answer." His voice is tight, clipped, the sound of a person backed into a corner. He shakes his head. "I still can't believe you did this without my permission."

My heart is a mix of gratitude for Gomo and shame for doing this to Appa. "Appa, I—"

He holds up a hand, stopping me. "Let's talk about this later."

I know him well enough to know that he's using all his effort to keep his voice under control. He walks out of the kitchen and disappears into his room with a click of the door. A high tide of guilt rises inside me. I cannot believe I just did that. He is so mad at me. But beneath the guilt, something glimmers like treasure at the bottom of a swimming pool.

I'm going to Korea.

I'm going to Korea!

I press my fist against my mouth and, despite myself, I smile.

KOREA PACKING LIST

- Clothes (check the weather in Korea to decide what to bring)
- Toiletries (toothbrush, toothpaste, floss, shampoo—or use the stuff at Gomo's?)
- Film camera
- Phone charger and adapters
- Headphones
- Journal
- Gift for Gomo (vitamins?)
- Plan to find my mom (to make on the plane)

Eight

The day I'm scheduled to fly out to Korea, Appa takes the morning off to drive me to the airport. I'm surprised. Ever since I bought the tickets, things have been extra weird between us and we've barely spoken all week. We never did talk more about it later like he said we would—the whole me going behind his back thing—though it feels like his anger has cooled off into a begrudging acceptance. A part of me is glad for it, but another part of me is disappointed. I thought maybe after I made a gesture this big, he would finally respond in some way, any way at all. But he doesn't, so I bury the feeling and try to just be grateful for the ride.

I have a backpack on my lap and one carry-on suitcase in the trunk with a luggage tag shaped like a honeydew looped through the handle. I don't know where that honeydew came from, just that it was already swinging from the suitcase when I pulled it out of storage. Maybe it came as a set. However it appeared, I'm glad it's there. It's small and silly, but the reality that I'm going to Korea to secretly look for my mom has made me feel queasier and queasier in the week leading up to today and the honeydew has felt like a mini anchor, something bright and green and tangible to pull me back to the task at hand when my thoughts were getting too loud. Just keep rolling your T-shirts. Just keep slotting them in.

"I haven't been on a plane in so long," I say. "Nikita gave me a list of movies I can watch, but I might just pass out the whole time. Too bad I don't have one of those neck pillows. I'll probably wake up with a sore neck from sleeping weird."

I'm rambling, half nervous energy, half trying to fill the awkwardness between us. Appa just nods.

Check-in at the airport is smooth. We have some extra time to kill before I have to go through the gate, so we go to the food court to grab a quick bite. We order burgers and baked potatoes at Wendy's.

"Be right back. Bathroom," Appa says, leaving me at a table with our plastic trays of food. "You can start eating."

"Okay." I scroll through my phone, making sure I have all my music downloaded for the flight. My leg is jittery under the table.

Appa comes back holding a shopping bag from the gift store. He puts it down in front of me and takes a seat.

"What's this?" I ask.

"Open it," he says.

I reach inside the bag and pull out a neck pillow. A lump forms in my throat. What is it about airports that makes you feel ten times more emotional about things than you might normally? Or maybe it's not the airport. Maybe it's just us.

There's so much I want to say, but I don't have the words.

"Thank you," I whisper.

He nods, spreading sour cream on his baked potato. I put the pillow around my neck and leave it there the whole time as we finish our meal.

One time I vanished during a school field trip. Here's what I remember about it: I was fourteen and we went kayaking at Granville Island. I was in a double kayak with a redheaded girl named Tamara. We were paddling out to False Creek, me in the back and Tamara in the front, when she turned around and said, "Sorry, I forgot to put on sunscreen. Give me a sec."

I remember thinking I should have put on sunscreen too. I remember it was sunny and hot and Tamara had big cat-eye sunglasses on top of her head that reflected the light. "Can I have some?"

"Sure." Tamara threw me the tube of sunscreen.

It smelled like coconut and pineapple and then, just like that, I wasn't in the boat anymore. Disappearance Number Five: I was in Nikita's kitchen. We were nine and making piña colada smoothies with her mom.

"This is my favorite drink ever," Nikita was saying, bouncing around the kitchen. "Mom, Aimee's never had piña colada before!"

"It's a super easy recipe," Mrs. Lai-Sanders said as she popped frozen pineapples into the blender. She smiled at me, warm. "I can give it to you if you like it and you can make it with your mom at home too."

Nikita stopped bouncing. "*Mom*," she said. "I told you."

Mrs. Lai-Sanders's face turned pink. "I mean, make it with your dad. Or, you know, even by yourself if you're allowed to use the blender on your own."

I could tell she felt bad so I laughed, a little too loud, and said, "Sure, that'd be great, thank you so much."

Nikita grabbed a packet of little umbrellas that she popped into the piña coladas after Mrs. Lai-Sanders poured them into glasses decorated with pink flamingos. They moved in a rhythmic way like they'd done this dozens of times before. Mrs. Lai-Sanders passed me a glass.

It smelled like summer. No wonder it was Nikita's favorite drink.

Four minutes and eleven seconds later, I reappeared in the boat. By then, Tamara had paddled farther out to False Creek by herself, but was going around in circles without me.

I remember feeling huge relief that day because it was when I learned that if I disappear while in a moving vehicle—a car, a train, or in this case a kayak—and the vehicle keeps moving without me, I'll reappear where I was sitting in the vehicle rather than reappearing in the exact spot I disappeared. For a long time, I had this fear that I would disappear while Appa was driving and then I would reappear in the middle of the road where I'd vanished, Appa and the car long gone, and then I would get hit by a startled driver. That's how I would die. Grim and unpredictable. But after this field trip, my mind was at ease. I still have fears about disappearing while I'm the one driving and causing an accident, but at least this specific scenario would never happen.

Lucky for me. If I had vanished where I'd started, I would have ended up popping back into the water.

I remember Tamara wasn't as lucky. She was so shocked by my sudden reappearance that she screamed and tipped right out of the kayak. Her cat-eye sunglasses fell off and sank into the water. "Why do you have to be such a freak?" she grumbled.

I remember going to the mall to buy her I'm-Sorry Sunglasses from Old Navy the next day.

As the plane takes off from YVR, I look out the window. I fog it up with my breath and draw a cat with the tip of my finger. My stomach's still in knots, but I'm doing this. I'm going to Korea. I'm looking for my mom. At least I know that if I vanish in the airplane, I won't reappear in the middle of the sky. Small comforts.

We climb higher and higher into the clouds. I lean back into my neck pillow and close my eyes.

About twelve hours later, we land at Incheon International Airport. I feel groggy. I was supposed to make my plan to find my mom on the plane, but I didn't get very far on that since I ended up just sleeping for most of the ride. This is off to a great start.

Gomo said she would be waiting for me at the gates. What I remember about Gomo: she came to stay with us for a few weeks after my mom left and she took care of everything. All of my memories of her are light leaked with sunshine. She cooked the best food, sang old Korean ballads while cleaning, and walked me to school, holding hands, swinging arms. She was so easy and fun to be around. When she left, I cried for days. I missed her so much that we went to go visit her in Korea the following year over summer break. She took time off to take me to Lotte World, the amusement park, and went on all the rides with me while Appa held our stuff.

Will she even recognize me now? It's been almost ten years. By the time I exit into Arrivals, the nervous energy I was feeling earlier in the car with Appa comes back twice as strong. I look around, uncertain, a man bumping into my shoulder and offering a quick apology before disappearing into the crowd of people. So many people. My hands feel clammy.

"Aimee!" a voice rings out. "Aimee! Over here!"

Snapshot: I am a boat, adrift in a sea of strangers speaking rapid Korean, my honeydew luggage tag the only thing keeping me afloat. And then: Gomo. She is a lighthouse. Beaming at me with the force of a thousand stars, arms waving in the air.

She looks just as I remember her, all smiles that make the corners of her eyes crinkle, dyed brown hair threatening to spring out of the messy bun on top of her head.

"Annyeonghaseyo, Gomo," I say, rushing over to her.

She wraps me in a hug. "It's been so long! You haven't forgotten all your Korean, have you?"

"Of course not," I reply in Korean.

"Good, because we have a lot to catch up on." She weaves her fingers through mine and leads me through the airport. Holding hands, swinging arms. We've been together for less than a minute and already it feels like no time has passed at all since I last saw her. "Let's get you rested at home! I can't believe how much you've grown!"

We get a SIM card for my phone at the airport before heading for the subway. Gomo already has a T-money card prepared for me, a reloadable card I can use to get on public transit, and shows me how to tap it at the subway station to get through the gates. The subways are a lot longer and bigger than the SkyTrains in Vancouver, and the map looks way more complicated too. There are dozens of different colored lines crisscrossing each other. Gomo explains it to me as best she can and downloads a subway map app onto my phone. "This will come in handy while you're here," she says. She also gets me to download Naver Maps, which she says is useful to navigate around Korea.

We transfer once and eventually get off at Mapo Station.

Gomo makes me star it in both my subway app and Naver Maps so I remember where home base is. Her apartment is about a ten-minute walk away from the station.

I want to take out my film camera and capture these first few moments in Korea—Gomo sitting in the subway, head leaning against the window, the walk to her place, the GS25 convenience store where we stop to buy ice cream bars. But I settle for taking quick snaps on my phone for now. It's 6:30 p.m. here, which means it's 2:30 a.m. in Vancouver. I'm barely keeping my eyes open by the time we get into Gomo's apartment, even though I slept so much on the plane.

Still, I catch a second wind and manage to stay awake for the amazing homemade dinner Gomo has prepared for me. Freshly grilled mackerel, cucumber kimchi, garlic chive pancakes, and gamja jorim, my favorite way ever to eat potatoes. She smiles at me the whole time we eat, but her smile is tinged with a little bit of sadness.

"Where did all the time go," she sighs. "You're already a young lady. I thought I'd have more time to visit you as a child before this happened." She reaches across the table and squeezes my hand, the sadness disappearing. "But I'm so glad you're here now."

There's that lump in my throat again. I swallow hard and squeeze back. "Me too, Gomo."

She sets me up in her guest bedroom, laying a stack of towels at the foot of the bed for me to use. I unpack a little and then get ready to sleep.

I check my phone as I brush my teeth, looking at the two separate messages I sent Appa and Nikita when I arrived at Incheon Airport. I wrote them both the same thing: *Made it to Korea!* They both replied right away.

Appa:

Okay.

Nikita:

AHHH YOU'RE IN KOREA! CAN YOU BELIEVE IT?

Nikita:

Remember, keep me updated on everything about the investigation.

Nikita:

I'm here to help!

Right. The investigation. I still have no idea how I'm going to pull this off, but for now, I tuck it to the back of my mind, too tired to do otherwise.

I send both Appa and Nikita a photo of the dinner Gomo made me. They'll be sleeping now, but they can see it when they wake up in the morning. I join them in sleep, crawling into bed.

Tomorrow, the investigation begins.

FROM THE PAGES OF AIMEE'S JOURNAL

Plan to find my mom:

Nine

My phone lights up at 5:00 a.m. with a message from Appa. I've already been awake for half an hour, sitting up in bed with my journal propped open in my lap, so I see it right away.

Appa:

Are you awake?

Me:

Yes.

My phone rings and I answer it.

"Hi, Appa."

"How's the jet lag?" he asks.

"It's only five a.m. here and I've been awake for a while. But it's not too bad. What time is it there?"

"One p.m."

"Ah."

There's a beat of silence where neither of us knows what to say next, and then he clears his throat and says, "I had a phone call with an old friend of mine this morning and he wants to treat you to lunch. He's in town with his son from Toronto. Would today work for you?"

Today? Today is supposed to be day one of my investigation. But how am I supposed to say that to Appa? *Sorry, I can't have lunch with your friend, I'm busy trying to secretly find my mom?* But then it hits me that maybe an old friend of Appa's is the best person to begin my investigation with. If he's known Appa for a long time, maybe he also knew my mom and he might be willing to talk.

"Today is good," I say.

"Okay. His name is Mr. Kim. You might remember him and Junho from our last trip to Korea? We met them then, but maybe you were too young."

"Junho?"

"His son. He's your age."

Wait. Junho. Junho Kim.

The connection clicks into place. "Are you talking about the Mr. Kim and Junho we had hoddeok with the last time we came to Korea?"

"I don't remember, but probably. That sounds about right."

Oh my god. Cute tattoo boy from the memory. I can't believe he's actually here in Korea at the same time as me. Nikita is going to lose it.

"I'll give Mr. Kim your contact. He'll message you," Appa says.

"Cool," I say faintly.

There's a pause and then he says, in Korean, "I'm hanging up now." A common expression, but it makes the air feel extra awkward between us. We say goodbye and hang up. I wonder if it will ever not be weird between us again. I thought we were distant before, but now add "buying a plane ticket to Korea behind his back" to the list of things we talk around and it's gotten even more strained. I'm starting to lose track of all the things we can't say.

I flop back in bed and think about seeing Junho again. I realize I didn't even ask if he would be joining today. Appa just said he was in town. He didn't necessarily say he'd be at lunch. But he also didn't say he *wouldn't* be at lunch.

I hug one of the giant pillows, burying my face in it, smiling.

Mr. Kim invites me to meet him this afternoon at a kalguksu restaurant in Myeongdong. Gomo gives me in-depth instructions on how to get there before leaving for work, an elementary school nearby where she teaches third graders. In Korea, the new school year begins in March, and I feel a little guilty for intruding in her space right at the start of a busy time, but she waves off my concern. "Please," she says. "You're being ridiculous!"

She has an early meeting today and leaves breakfast for me in the kitchen. Fresh rice in the rice cooker and mu guk on the stove.

It's different from the bowl of cereal Appa and I always eat together in the mornings. But I like it. The radish soup is warm and soothing and I finish every bite before doing the dishes. And then I slowly get ready. A black knit sweater tucked into a pair of black wide-leg pants with a red scarf tied in my hair. I grab my camera and my journal, shove them all into my tote bag, and head out to Myeongdong.

Seoul. It's hard to believe I'm really here. I have memories of visiting as a kid, but it's different being older and going around by myself. I wonder if I blend in. Or if I stand out.

I successfully make it to Myeongdong, Naver Maps open on my phone the whole time. At once it is overwhelming. The streets are busy with people, even during daytime on a weekday, and there are stores in every direction I look. Gomo told me Myeongdong is a popular shopping area for tourists, but I feel like that's an understatement. Employees stand outside beauty stores, calling out to people in Korean, English, Mandarin, and Japanese, ushering them inside. "Come in, come in! There's a twenty percent off sale today. You don't want to miss it!"

Amazing smells tug at me from left and right as I weave my way through food stalls—deep-fried everything, twigim and mandu, chicken skewers, ice cream so tall it looks like it's reaching for heaven—and I'm caught between the thrill of wanting to see it all and the uneasiness that any one of these scents might pitch me back. I imagine disappearing in the middle of all these people, reappearing in a huge crowd of tourists, all stopping to stare at me. My grip on my tote bag tightens.

"Why don't you just avoid scents that you think might take you back?" classmates have asked me in the past. "Or just wear a nose plug and not smell things at all?"

They say it like it's the easiest thing in the world. *Why don't you just stop?* Because it's really so simple to remember all the scents you've encountered in your life and to prepare for the exact moment you might come across them again. Never mind the fact that it's not a sure thing which scent will be a trigger and which won't.

Besides, I don't want to live afraid of everything.

And yet.

I hurry past the food stalls and makeup stores and make my way to the kalguksu restaurant, keeping my head down, holding my breath despite myself.

I'm a bit early. Mr. Kim and I agreed to meet right outside the kalguksu place, so I wait. The restaurant is already bustling, the door swinging open again and again as people walk in for lunch, bellies hungry for noodles. My fingers itch to grab my camera, but I figure it's not a good look to be loitering outside a restaurant, taking pictures of strangers coming through the door. I capture them in my mind instead.

Snapshot: a couple in matching striped long sleeves, arms so linked together that they look almost like one person approaching the restaurant, not two. They enter.

Snapshot: a boy in wireless headphones, so lost in whatever he's listening to that he looks almost bewildered to have ended up at the restaurant at all, like the wind carried him here by chance. Maybe it did. He nearly bumps into me, smiling an apology, a quick bow of the head. He enters.

Snapshot: a group of businessmen, voices loud and raucous, neckties in varying shades of blue. I jump one image ahead, picture them tucking napkins into their collars as they sit around the table. Protect the ties at all costs! They enter.

"Is this Aimee?"

I turn from my watch of the door to see a bald Korean man with clear-rimmed glasses perched on top of his head walking toward me, waving a hand in the air. He looks older than Appa, closer to maybe Gomo's age, and when he smiles, he looks positively jolly. This must be Mr. Kim.

"Annyeonghaseyo." I bow in greeting.

"It's been a long time! Welcome to Korea," he says, using a mix of English and Korean like I do with Appa. He chuckles. "Not that I live here anymore either. Just visiting. Funny that we both live in Canada but ended up meeting here, huh?"

I laugh and take a quick peek behind him. No Junho. Seems like Mr. Kim came alone. Too bad I won't have a story for Nikita after all. I swallow down my quiet disappointment, but quickly recover.

"Shall we go inside?" I say, reaching for the door.

"Thank you," he says, stepping inside. We're instantly greeted by the sound of chatter and laughter, slurping noodles, shouted orders. Mr. Kim puts on his glasses and squints across the restaurant. "My son is joining us. He said he's got a table. Ah, there he is!"

My stomach flips as I follow his gaze to a boy sitting in the corner, headphones around his neck. He sees his dad, waves. And then he sees me, recognition lighting his eyes.

The boy who bumped into me outside, the one I took a mental snapshot of. *That's* Junho? I can't believe I didn't realize it was him. I mean, of course I wouldn't. It's been a decade. But also, I thought that maybe there would be this instant knowing between us like . . . *soul mates*, a voice in my head says, sounding suspiciously like Nikita.

I inwardly roll my eyes at myself. Just because you have a crush on someone as a kid doesn't make them your soul mate.

Even so, my stomach keeps on doing strange things as Mr. Kim leads me to the table. "Aimee, you remember my son, Junho," he says. "Or do you? It's been a long time."

"I remember," I say, too quiet. Does he remember me too?

"Hi," Junho says with a wave. His teeth are a little crooked, his hair flattened from where the headphones pressed it down. I wonder what he was listening to earlier that made it look like he was dreaming. He looks totally alert now.

We order. Mr. Kim is talking about something, but every few seconds my eyes trail over to sneak a glance at Junho. I can't believe he's actually here. Things hardly ever happen in real life the way I imagine them in my head. He catches me staring at him and tilts his head to the side, smiling at me curiously. My cheeks go warm and I quickly look away.

Moments later, bowls of knife-cut noodles topped with green onions and dumplings swimming in a warm soul-filling broth appear before us, along with slabs of kimchi on side plates.

"Jal meokgetseumnida," we say before digging in. The flavor is amazing, momentarily chasing all other thoughts out of my brain. I'm certain I could eat this every day and never get sick of it.

"What do you think?" Mr. Kim asks.

"It's so good," I say.

"Minho would love this. Kalguksu's his favorite," Junho says, lifting a long string of noodles with his chopsticks. He looks at me and adds, "Minho's my younger brother."

"Is he here in Korea too?" I ask.

"No, he lives in Calgary with my mom."

"Slow down before you choke, will you?" Mr. Kim says as Junho takes a huge bite of noodles.

Junho slows down, taking a sip of tea.

"So how's your dad?" Mr. Kim asks.

"He's good," I answer. I know it's not the right word exactly, but I'm not sure what else to say.

Mr. Kim shakes his head. "I can't believe he didn't come with you to Korea. It's been ages since I've last seen him!"

"How do you two know each other?" I ask.

"Actually, I was friends with your aunt first. We were the same grade and she would let her kid brother tag along whenever we hung out." He laughs. "He was annoying. Would never shut up."

"Really?" I try to picture Appa as a kid, talking the ears off Gomo and Mr. Kim. It's hard to imagine. Impossible almost.

"Oh yeah. But he became like my own brother over time." At this, he looks regretful. "I should have checked in more over the years. Tried to visit you both in Vancouver. But time just kept getting away from me. Immigrating to Toronto, working, having kids, life changes . . . the days just went by too fast. Not that it's any excuse. I know it hasn't been an easy time for him, or you, for that matter."

I glance at Junho, whose eyes are fixated on his nearly empty bowl. I wonder how much he knows about me. About my family. About my disappearing.

I look back to Mr. Kim, trying to figure out how to segue this conversation into what I want to know. "Were you close with my mom too?" I ask.

Subtle, Aimee. Very subtle.

"Your mom, not so much," Mr. Kim says. "I never got to know her too well. She was quite reserved, should I say? But they were together since early high school, so of course

I saw her around sometimes."

Oh. Interesting. I actually never knew they were together since high school, never even knew how they first met. I keep my face casual, afraid that if I show too much interest, he might stop talking.

"What kind of things did they do for fun back then? Them, or, you know, Korean teens in general." I keep it broad, general, playing it cool.

"Fun? They studied, that's what they did," Mr. Kim laughs. "Maybe play some sports. Watch a movie if there's time. Oh, and your mom's family owned a flower shop that she worked part-time at. Your dad would go there a lot to help out and try to impress her."

"What was the flower shop called?" I ask.

"Oh, what was it?" Mr. Kim snaps his fingers, trying to remember. "Um, I think it was . . . Dream a Dream Flowers! Yes, that's what it was."

Dream a Dream Flowers. I commit the name to memory as Mr. Kim starts talking about the sports he used to play as a teenager. We finish our kalguksu and he excuses himself to use the restroom and pay. As soon as he's gone, Junho, who's been fairly quiet during this conversation, turns to me with a raised eyebrow.

"So, two questions for you," he says, holding up two fingers. "Number one, why were you grilling my dad?"

My mouth drops open. "Me? Grilling? I was not."

"Really? Because it sounded like you were ready to shine

a light in his eyes to get some answers," he says, teasing.

So much for playing it cool. "I was just curious."

He waits for me to continue, like he knows there's more to the story. But what is there to say? The truth is too personal, too absurd. "I'm working on an art project," I say instead, the lie falling from my lips.

At this, his eyes spark with interest. "An art project? Tell me more."

"It's a . . . photography project," I say, stalling. "Where I take pictures."

He smiles. "I assumed."

"It's kind of like a family tree project. But instead of pictures of my actual family members, I'm capturing places and things that were important to them throughout their life. And I figure, what better time and place to do that than here in Korea, where they lived for so long?"

Wow. Not bad for something I came up with on the spot. In another circumstance, this might have been a project I would actually be interested in.

Junho leans forward in his seat. "That sounds so cool. I'd love to help."

"You—what?"

"I mean, only if you want help, of course. Like if you need an assistant to carry your equipment. Or if you need help scoping out locations? Sorry, I don't want to butt in." He laughs sheepishly. "But I've mostly been hanging out with my dad while we're here and it'd be nice to hang out with someone who's not him. I mean, don't get me wrong, he's cool and it's been great. But I just want to do more things with more people, you know?"

Um. Honestly, I don't know. I can't imagine why he would want to do more things with more people when he could just as easily do things by himself. But I get the sense that Junho is much more of an extrovert than I am and settle for a shrug.

"It's kind of a personal project," I say.

"Ah, okay. I understand." He looks disappointed and I feel bad, but not quite bad enough to take it back. And then he perks up. "You know I'm an artist too?"

"You are?"

"Yeah. An illustrator. I want to make webtoons one day."

"What are webtoons?"

"You don't know webtoons? They're digital comics that originated here in Korea." He pulls out his phone and opens up the Webtoon app, showing it to me. "See? Anyone can publish their stories on Webtoon. There are a bunch of comics you can read right here on your phone. Some of them are really huge. They have millions of reads."

"Wow, that's very cool." I'm about to ask him what kind of stories he wants to create when Mr. Kim calls to us from the cash register where he's finished paying. He waves us over to leave.

Junho rises, grabbing his jacket from the back of his chair.

"What was your second question?" I ask, standing as

well. "You said you have two."

"Oh yeah." Now that we're standing side by side, I can see how tall he is. When we were seven, I was definitely the taller one. Now I have to look up to meet his gaze. He grins. "Why'd you keep staring at me during lunch?"

My cheeks go warm again, burning. "Me? Stare at you? I wasn't."

"Oh? I thought I saw you."

"Nope. Not me. And if I did, it's only because you have something on your face. Right there, see?"

I point at a vague general direction on his face. He lifts his hand, brushing his cheek with his fingers and looking down at them.

"Did I get it?" he asks, eyes flickering back to me, the corner of his lip quirking up.

My head goes empty, all the words I ever knew in my life flying out of my brain. "Mhm," I manage.

Mr. Kim calls for us again and Junho looks away, heading toward his dad. I exhale slowly, gathering myself, and then hurry to catch up with him. I might regret what I'm about to do, but in the moment, I make a quick decision and go with my gut.

"You know," I say, speaking in a rush before I can take it back. "I don't need an assistant for my project, but you can tag along with me if you want. Work on your art while I work on mine?"

He smiles, his whole face lighting up. "Really? That

sounds great. Only if you're sure you're cool with it. We should swap numbers!"

Something defensive prickles in my mind. A voice that says *you don't really know him* and *are you sure this is a good idea* and *the fewer people who get involved in this the better.* But in the moment, the unease gets swallowed up by his warmth.

So he'll be with me while I look for clues to find my mom. No big deal. I don't have to tell him anything I don't want to share. As far as he's concerned, it's just a photography project. And maybe that's a good way for me to look at it too. Maybe it'll take some pressure off this whole thing, calling it an art project instead of an investigation.

After all, an art project has limitless potential. And I need to believe in that right now.

"Okay." I pull out my phone, opening a New Contact page. A giddy feeling flutters in my stomach as I pass it to Junho, knowing that I'll get to see him again. "Let's do it."

KAKAO MESSENGER

Junho:

Hi it's Junho! Thought we could chat here about your project.

Aimee:

Hi! So I'm thinking of starting tomorrow at the flower shop your dad was telling me about today . . .

Aimee:

Do you want to join? If you want to ofc. It might be boring for you.

Junho:

I'll be there. I love flowers.

Aimee:

Really?

Junho:

Oh for sure. Flower enthusiast over here.

Aimee:

Yeah? What kind of flowers do you like?

Junho:

Um . . . yellow ones?

Aimee:

Very enthusiast of you.

Junho:

What about you? What kind do you like?

Aimee:

Hmm I like . . . forget-me-nots?

Junho:

Oh yeah. Those are great. Very pretty.

Aimee:

. . .

Junho:

. . .

Aimee:

You're googling what they look like right now, aren't you?

Junho:

Sorry but we just met, you're not allowed to see through me like that yet.

Aimee:

Hahaha. See you tomorrow then?

Junho:

See you :)

Ten

The next day is Tuesday and Junho and I have plans to go to the flower shop. Dream a Dream Flowers is easy to find on Naver Maps. There's only one shop of that name in Seoul, and judging by the description boasting that it's been around for the past forty years, I have hope that it might be the same one that my mom's family ran.

Maybe even still runs.

I imagine walking in and seeing my mom behind the counter, arranging roses. What are the chances? What would I say? Or maybe my grandparents would be the ones still there, running the store. I've never met them before so they wouldn't know me. What if today is the first day we meet?

What if what if what if?

"So tell me more about your photography project," Junho says. We walk from the subway station we met at, me navigating on my phone, him following my lead. It's sunny but brisk. He's wearing black jeans and a faded blue hoodie, a sketchbook tucked in the crook of his arm, the same headphones from yesterday looped around his neck. Our arms bump against each other as we walk. I wonder if he's doing it on purpose. I don't stop him if he is.

"How about you tell me more about your webtoons first?" I say. "I got curious about it after you showed me yesterday and started reading one."

"Oh yeah?" He grins. "Which one?"

"*Tower of God*. I like it so far. It was one of the top recommended."

"That's a huge one. It's one of my favorites too. Okay. Trade a fact for a fact, then?"

I hesitate and then nod. "Fair."

"I've loved drawing since I was a kid. And I've been obsessed with comic books and manga and manhwa forever. It was only a matter of time before I started wanting to make my own."

"I remember that," I say without thinking. He raises his eyebrows and I clear my throat. "I mean the drawing part. I remember that from when we met as kids. You drew pretend tattoos on yourself."

"Oh yeah." His grin widens. "Didn't I draw one for you too?"

"Maybe."

We pass by coffee shops, convenience stores, and a restaurant chain selling dak galbi, a spicy chicken stir-fry shared out of a huge pan. It's a quieter area here than in Myeongdong, especially when we turn into an alley, the bigger shops and restaurants giving way to smaller hole-in-the-wall places specializing in single items—candles, kimbap, secondhand shoes.

"I used to make mini comic books for my younger brother," he says. "I'd make up superheroes for him, like Super Bean, who was born from a can struck by magic lightning. Kid stuff like that. He loved it."

I laugh, picturing Junho with a serious, focused face, drawing a picture of a bean in a superhero costume. "Your brother's name is Minho, right? You said he lives in Alberta?"

"Yeah. My parents got divorced when we were kids, so he lives in Calgary with our mom and I live in Toronto with our dad. He just turned thirteen."

"I see," I say, nodding. "Is it hard living apart? It sounds like you were close."

"Yeah, we were. Still are. It can be tough." His expression turns a bit cloudy, but then he smiles and it's gone as quickly as it came. "I believe it's your turn to offer a fact?"

"Right. Um . . . I like film photography. I got into it because we had a film camera at our house." I pause, and then add, "It was my mom's."

"Ah." He nods, turning to look at me while he talks. His face is open, gentle. "My dad told me about your mom. I hope it's okay that I know?"

"Oh. Yeah. It's not a secret or anything. And she left a long time ago." I say it in a rush, laughing a little, as if I'm not in the middle of actively trying to find her right now. I reach for something else to say but find nothing, change the topic instead. "Your turn. And I have a question for you actually."

"Shoot."

"Do you have a webtoon up already?" I don't mention that I already tried searching his name on the site last night to see if he posted anything. He didn't, or at least not under a name that I could find.

"Not yet. My dad doesn't believe I can make a good comic."

"He doesn't support you?"

"Oh, he's supportive of my art. I'm planning on going to OCAD in the fall—that's an art school in Toronto, if you haven't heard of it—and he's all proud about that. But he thinks I'm a terrible writer. And honestly, he's not wrong." He laughs. "I never have any decent story ideas. Been trying to come up with something for ages. I'm waiting for one that my dad won't roast me for before putting it online. He's like my biggest fan and my worst critic."

I laugh too. What might it be like to have that kind of relationship with your dad? I try to imagine Appa as my biggest fan, but I'm not sure what that would even look like. Worst critic is easier to imagine.

"Maybe you'll find some inspiration today," I say.

His arm brushes against mine again and he catches my gaze, smiling. "Maybe. I do feel lucky today."

My stomach swoops a little, the way he says it. Lucky?

Does he mean because of me? "Or you could always bring back Super Bean," I add.

"I could always bring back Super Bean," he agrees.

We pause for a second as I check my map, make sure we're going the right way. The flower shop should be coming up soon.

"What do you like about film photography?" Junho asks.

"Hmm. I like how much time it takes," I say. I touch the film camera hanging against my chest, its weight tugging at the strap around my neck. "The whole process of developing the photos myself. Seeing the images appear on a blank piece of photo paper. In the darkroom, it's just me, in my element, involved in every step of the process from beginning to end, creating something from nothing."

"Sounds like a holy experience," he says.

The word makes me pause. *Holy*. It rings true somewhere deep in my gut. If ever there was a sanctuary for me, it would be the darkroom; if ever a sacred moment, the breath between a photo being not yet and then here, slowly appearing on the page.

"Yes," I say.

"Art's kind of amazing in that way, huh?" He has that dreamy look on his face again, the same one I saw when he was just a stranger walking into a kalguksu restaurant. It makes me wish I could see what he's seeing. "For me, making art is when I feel the most present and grounded.

And, this is going to sound so cheesy, but the most me?" He stops walking, smiles at me, and nudges my shoulder with his. "What a couple of art nerds, huh?"

My heart does a funny thing, a kind of stuttering like it's been seen in a way it wasn't expecting and doesn't know what to do with its hands. "Yeah," I say, and look down at my phone, checking the map.

We've totally passed the flower shop.

I sheepishly redirect us backward and this time, we find it. Dream a Dream Flowers. It's modest and small, but kept in excellent condition, a fresh coat of white paint glistening on the sign, beautiful bouquets lined up in the window.

"Businesses in Korea change really fast," Junho says. "It's amazing that they're still up and running. Do you know if your mom's family still owns it?"

My heart thuds in my chest for a completely different reason now. Up until this moment, it was all hypothetical, finding my mom, gaining some closure, figuring out if she has STWS like me. But she could be on the other side of this door at this very moment. I could ask her all my questions, find all my answers. Suddenly, I'm not so sure this was the right thing to do, but I've come this far. I can't go back now.

"We'll see," I say, and I push the door open.

A middle-aged woman stands behind a long table, arranging a bouquet of flowers. Unlike the serene vibe of the store, the woman looks frenzied, jabbing flowers into the arrangement, hair flying out of her ponytail. The moment I see her, my stomach sinks.

She's not my mom.

I'm disappointed and relieved all at once.

"Can I help you?" she asks, looking up from her arrangement. Her eyes shift to Junho. "You're not Shim Taesung coming to pick up your bouquet, are you?"

"Um, no, I'm not," Junho says.

"Good, because I told him multiple times it wouldn't be ready till four p.m." She wipes her hands on her apron. "What can I do for you two students?"

"Just browsing, thank you," Junho says. He flips opens his sketchbook and starts meandering around the flowers on display. I approach the lady and lower my voice, hoping he won't hear.

"I'm looking for a Baek Youngmi?" I say, uncertain. "Does she still work here? Her family used to own this shop."

"Ah, you're talking about the daughter of the previous shop owners," the woman says in recognition. She shakes her head. "Sorry. They sold the store a while ago. We just kept the name."

My disappointment grows larger, eclipsing the relief I felt earlier.

A dead end. Of course it wouldn't be so easy to find her. I can't believe I even thought that I would.

"Thank you very much," I say.

I turn to leave when Junho tugs gently on my elbow.

"Aren't you going to take a photo for your project?" he whispers.

Oh right. The project. I smile meekly and ask the woman if it's okay to take a photo. She nods and I point my camera at the front counter, where the sun is catching dust motes in the air. I picture my mom in the frame, a teenager with flowers in her arms, a young Appa leaning against a broomstick, keeping her company. Peonies, roses, baby's breath between them.

I snap the photo.

Junho and I walk back to the subway station in silence. My brain feels foggy, pulling away from everything around me and circling the dead end at the flower shop, over and over again. *Of course she wasn't there. Why did I think she would be here?* Junho keeps glancing at me like he can tell something's wrong but doesn't know what to say. Eventually, I manage a small smile at him, breaking the silence.

"Today was fun. Thanks for coming with me."

He tilts his head to the side. "Yeah? You sure everything's okay? You seem . . . a little sad."

I shake my head. "I'm good."

He looks doubtful. "Sounds like my brother when he says he's all good."

"Why? You don't believe him when he says that?"

"There's always something going on with him."

"Not me," I say. I really did enjoy my day with him and I don't want to drag him down by being gloomy now. We get to the subway platform and I point left. "I go this way."

"I'm the opposite," he says. There's a musical jingle in the station, signaling that his subway is about to pull in. "Want to see what I drew?" he asks in a rush.

I nod. He opens his sketchbook, revealing a page of flowers. He's drawn all kinds at different angles, some elegantly shaded, some loosely scribbled, some in one long flowing line, never lifting from the page. All beautiful like a garden pressed to paper. And, in the middle of the page, there's one single real flower, a tiny sprig of forget-me-not.

"It fell off one of the bouquets while I was drawing," he says. He plucks it from the page and holds it out to me with a grin. "I picked it up off the floor. It's still as good as new, but it would have been swept away into the trash by the end of the day so I thought I'd save it from its unfortunate demise."

"And you're giving your rescue to me?"

"I am. I'm generous. Someone told me it's your favorite."

I take the sprig, delicate between my fingers. "It is. Thank you. It's pretty."

"I thought so too." He looks at me and smiles.

I smile back, face warm. "I think your subway's about to leave."

"Oh! Right!" He glances at his subway sitting there with its doors open and jogs backward, waving at me. "See you soon, right?"

I laugh. "Watch where you're going!"

The doors slide shut as he bumps right into someone. He bows profusely in apology and then grins at me through the window, waving at me as his subway speeds away.

At first, I think I'll spend the rest of the day at home, dwelling in the disappointment of the flower shop, but after Gomo gets off work, she invites me to go to the shijang with her. So I do.

It's a welcome distraction. The outdoor marketplace is bustling with people. Similar to Myeongdong, there are multiple scents competing for my attention—the fishiness of dried anchovies for sale, the sweet smell of strawberries, perfectly in season, something deep-fried and delightful wafting from my left. The marketplace is all movement and color and sensory overload.

I cling on to the back of Gomo's shirt like a child, willing myself not to disappear. Ever since the flower shop visit, I've been feeling extra sensitive, and I know how stress can heighten my STWS. Gomo knows about my condition, but she's never seen it happen before. If I disappear here, she would probably get so worried.

If I disappear here, I'd probably reappear right on top of someone when I return, spilling their groceries everywhere.

If I disappear here—

"Here!" Gomo stops abruptly in front of a stall selling ddeokbokki. "Let's have a snack. You're okay with spicy food, right?"

The smell of the spicy stir-fried rice cakes coated in a thick glaze fills my nostrils. Around me, the marketplace thrums. People holler and laugh, the sound of wheels on carts towing produce rattling along the pavement. I'm still here. I exhale.

"I love spicy food," I say.

"Good, because the ddeokbokki here is my favorite," she says. She orders two servings and we take a seat at the stall's countertop table, pulling back the plastic chairs to sit.

I look around the shijang, silently observing. "Gomo, do you know if my parents came here a lot when they were younger?" I ask. Now that I know that Appa and my mom met in high school, I'm betting Gomo can answer some of the questions on my mind. She would have been around for their relationship after all. She might even be able to give me some clues on what I should do next since I struck out at the flower shop.

"Oh yeah," she says easily. "Your parents were all about these marketplaces. They were so young when they met so it's not like they had a lot of money. The way your dad would try to impress your mom by buying her cheap meals at the shijang!"

She laughs and I cling on to every word. "What else did they like to do?" I ask.

"Hmm, well. I don't remember much, but I do remember your mom loved the Han River, so your dad would sometimes take her out on those pedal boats you can rent there."

Pedal boats at the Han River. I commit the fact to memory as the stall owner places two steaming-hot plates of ddeokbokki in front of us accompanied by napkins and toothpicks.

"Mani meogeo, Aimee," Gomo says, patting my back. She definitely doesn't need to tell me twice to eat a lot. It looks delicious. She stabs a piece of rice cake with the toothpick and pops it in her mouth. "Ah ddeugeowo! Be careful, it's hot."

I blow on the ddeokbokki, steam coiling in the air, and take a bite. It's still hot, but it tastes so, so good. I swallow, thinking carefully about what to say next. "Mr. Kim said they were together since early high school."

"That's right." Gomo shakes her head. "I still can't believe Kim Sungmin is in town and took you out for lunch but didn't even call me. The talking-to I gave him on the phone after you told me! What kind of friend are you, I said. He now owes me two lunches."

I laugh and then grow quiet, looking down at my food. "They were together for a long time, huh? My parents."

"Yes. It's too bad about how it all ended." Gomo sighs, shaking her head, and gives me a small, sympathetic smile. "Of course, it's not my place to say. You're the one who lived it. You've been through so much."

I don't know what to say but all of a sudden, there's a lump in my throat.

"Do you know?" I ask, putting down my toothpick. "Why she left?"

She shakes her head again. "Only very generally, though you should probably hear it from your dad, not me. It might not be my place to share."

So Appa does know more than he's let on. I sigh inwardly. How do I explain to Gomo that there's close to zero chance I'll ever hear it from him directly?

"I never knew your mom very well," Gomo continues. "We never went deeper than the surface-level greetings. Maybe I should have tried more, but there was always this distance between us, like she lived behind a wall I could never cross over. I suppose you could say your dad spent his life scaling that wall. He would do just about anything to make her laugh." She twirls a piece of ddeokbokki on her toothpick, lost in thought. "In fact, he would challenge himself to stuff as many of these in his mouth as he could just to make her smile. He was the goofiest kid."

"He did that?"

Appa? Goofy? I can't picture it, just like I couldn't picture him as the kid who would follow Gomo and Mr. Kim around, annoying them with all his talking.

"Are you sure that was my dad?" I ask.

Gomo just laughs, finishing her ddeokbokki.

THINGS I KNOW

- My mom's name is Baek Youngmi.
- She lived behind a wall.
- My dad used to be the kind of person who would do anything to make her laugh.
- Maybe when she went away, she took all his laughter with her too.

Eleven

Swan boat rentals at the Han River are 15,000 won for forty minutes if you want to pedal and 20,000 won if you want the automated boat that you can steer. It's Wednesday afternoon and Junho and I choose the classic pedal option, donning our life jackets and launching out into the water in our swan-shaped boat. But ten minutes into our ride, I'm seriously regretting our decision.

"Aimee, I have a confession," Junho says.

"What is it?"

"If I knew that I would be embarrassing myself like this when you invited me to go to the Han River, I would have said no." He wheezes, wiping the sweat off his forehead with the back of his hand. "I haven't exercised like this in years."

"Honestly? Same. Take a break?"

"Please."

We stop pedaling and float in our swan boat, leaning back in our plastic seats and giving our legs a rest. I sneak a look at the side of his face, hesitating for a second before leaning my knee against his, just slightly, holding my breath.

He leans back, knee resting against knee, and I exhale quietly, smiling down at my hands.

Junho lets out a happy sigh. "I love being on the water."

"Even when you have to pedal a swan around?"

"I think it's technically a duck."

"Really?" I stick my head out of the open window and try to look at the boat from the outside. "This is a duck?"

"Yeah. Ori bae. Duck boat. It was on the signs and everything." He grins. "Why? Is it less appealing when it's a duck and not a swan?"

"I just always thought boats that looked like this were called swan boats," I say. "Not swan duck boats."

"Just duck boat," he corrects me.

"Swan duck," I repeat. He laughs.

I look out the window, scanning the waters at the other boats passing us by. After Gomo told me yesterday that Appa and my mom used to do this, I texted Junho and asked him if he'd like to join me at the river today as a stop on my photography project. I know the probability is highly unlikely that I'll actually find my mom here, but I keep my eyes out anyway. What if she passes me in a boat? Or I see her jogging along the river?

More than actually believing that I'll find her here, I wanted to ride in the boat to do what she did, to be close to her in a way that I didn't know how to be before. There's so little I know of her. I close my eyes as we bob in the water. My mom loved the Han River. I try to imagine Appa pedaling her around on a boat just like this one. It's hard to picture.

Junho's phone rings and I open my eyes. "Sorry, my brother's FaceTiming me," he says, throwing me a quick smile. "I just have to take this."

I gesture for him to go ahead, and he answers the call. Minho appears on-screen. It looks like he's walking down a sidewalk, gripping a backpack over one shoulder. Beneath his shaggy hair, he has an impish face, his mouth turned down in a sullen grimace.

"What's with the life jacket, Hyung?" he asks.

"I'm on a swan duck," Junho says. I stifle a laugh.

"Uh, okay."

"Where are you going?"

"I'm running away from home."

"What?!" Junho exclaims. He shoots me a glance and then looks around the boat, realizing there's nowhere for him to go to take this call in private. "Give me a second." He puts on the headphones looped around his neck and I turn away, looking out the window and pretending I can't hear anything to try to give him some semblance of privacy.

I try not to listen, but it's hard when you're floating in a river in a swan duck together. Junho asks his brother why he's running away, clearly trying to keep the distress in his voice as level as possible. He tries to convince him to go back for now, and gradually, from the relief in his tone, it sounds like he's able to convince him.

"I'll talk to Umma, okay? Hyung will take care of this," Junho says. "Okay. Yeah, okay. Text me when you're home. Talk to you soon."

He hangs up and takes off his headphones. "Sorry about that," he says.

"Hmm? Oh no, don't worry about me, I was just looking out the window," I say, gesturing to the water.

He raises an eyebrow. "Oh yeah? So you didn't hear anything?"

"Nope."

"But if I wanted to tell you about it, you'd listen, right?"

We slowly start pedaling again, the swan duck boat moving through the water. "If you wanted to, I'd listen," I say.

"Minho and my mom, they fight a lot," he says, keeping his eyes out to the river in front of him. "Actually, everyone in my family fights a lot. There's always something my parents are arguing about, and if they're not arguing, their favorite thing to do is complain about each other. And then there's my brother, who neither of them knows how to deal with. He gets into a lot of fights at school and spends most of his time feeling like they don't get him, which they totally don't. I'm kind of the peacekeeper of the family. It's my job to fix things when stuff like this happens. But you know what?" He sighs, leaning his head back against the seat and turning to look at me. "Sometimes I'd rather just float in a duck like this."

I look back at him, holding his eyes, hoping it carries

everything I want to say. *That sounds tough* and *thank you for sharing with me* and *sometimes I'd rather just float too.* But his gaze is so intense that my tongue gets tied and I break eye contact first, clearing my throat. "You mean swan duck," I say. I inwardly face-palm. That's not what I wanted to say.

He laughs. "Yeah. Swan duck."

We keep pedaling, and I rack my brain for a way to backtrack. "If you ever want to talk about anything more, I'll listen again," I blurt out.

He smiles at me, warm and bright. "Thanks."

Our time in the boat is up and we slowly pedal back to the dock to return it. It's only when we step out that I remember I have to take a picture for my pretend project. I pull out my film camera as Junho goes to return our life jackets and I snap a photo of the row of boats bobbing in the water.

First time in a swan duck boat, I think. That's a first I never thought I'd have.

Junho calls my name and I tuck my camera away, running to join him.

They say one of the prettiest places to watch the sunset is at the Han River.

Nikita will be so disappointed that I'm watching it alone, but Junho had to leave early to take care of his family matters, and honestly, I don't mind. As much as I've enjoyed my time with him and with Gomo, it feels good being alone like this. I need this time just to myself.

I set up my mat, an old dotjari that I brought with me from Gomo's place, and sit on the grass in the river park. I stretch my legs out in front of me and watch the sun begin to sink.

I think about my time in Korea so far. I haven't disappeared once since coming here. Maybe things are different for me in a new city. Or maybe in some way, by going to the places that my mom went and doing the things that she did, I'm finding that closure Hassan talked about. Then again, it's only been about four days. And I still have so many questions.

Besides, I can feel it. The uneasiness, lingering always just beneath the surface. Last night in bed, I was scrolling through the STWS forums, reading a thread called "Anyone else feel like they'll disappear at any moment? How do you deal?"

pinkzeebra56: *I feel this way all the time. The more I worry about disappearing, the more I feel like I disappear. Am I doing it to myself?*

hi_yourlocalsandwichgirl: *I don't deal lol.*

LilyyyM: *I've been there and it'll get better one day. I'll pray for you.*

NotARobot_11: *Meditation has helped me . . . but sometimes when the feeling is too heavy, I just accept that it is what it is and I have to go through it until it's over.*

It was almost as if the commenter had taken the words

right out of my head. *The more I worry about disappearing, the more I feel like I disappear. Am I doing it to myself?* I've been wondering that a lot. Is it me? Am I the problem? Is my brain just broken? Maybe there are no signs or bigger meanings. Maybe I'm just stressing myself into vanishing more. Appa always says that I have to be strong enough to resist it. Maybe I'm just too weak, and if I really was strong enough to stop thinking about it, it would go away by itself.

Maybe.

There's an STWS meetup happening in Seoul later this week. The timing is perfect if I want to go, but I'm not sure if I do. After my last meetup experience, I definitely feel wary. At the same time, I feel bolder than I have in a while. I got myself to Korea and now I'm out here doing new things, looking for my mom, eating ddeokbokki in a shijang, and riding a boat down the river with a boy who makes me smile. If there's going to be any time for me to give these meetups a second chance, it would be here.

The temptation is strong. How nice would it be to have other people to relate to about this? Especially here, especially now. Sometimes I don't even know what I'm looking for or how to put my feelings into words until I read a comment that makes me want to cry and shout, *Yes! That's what it is. That's how it feels.*

But still, strangers are strangers. I can hardly open up to my closest friends. And I'm still not even sure if Junho knows I have STWS.

My thoughts drift back to my mom. If she does have STWS, she could be the someone I talk to. The someone who might help me feel like I'm not so alone.

But then again, at this point, would she be any closer to me than a stranger on the internet?

My mind goes around and around, chasing itself in circles.

Snapshot: the sun is gone, tucked away into the Han River. The girl on the dotjari closes her eyes and tries to picture it rising again. She's not sure if she can see it yet. One day she hopes she can be someone who can see the sunrise in her mind.

KAKAO MESSENGER

Aimee:

Hey, thanks again for coming with me today!

Aimee:

Also sorry but is your new profile picture a photo of you with the swan duck boat?

Junho:

Please have some respect. His name is Gerald.

Aimee:

Rude of you not to introduce me properly while we were together today.

Junho:

He called me afterward to officially tell me his name. I think he likes me?

Aimee:

You're lucky. He's a very handsome swan duck.

Junho:

Hahaha.

Junho:

Btw I know this doesn't have anything to do with your project, but do you want to hang out with me and my friends tomorrow?

Junho:

They're in town and we're going to Seoul Forest. I promise snacks and good times with moderately cool people.

Aimee:

Haha sure why not? You sold me on the "moderately cool people."

Junho:

Yess!!

Junho:

Wait a minute dld you just change your profile picture to you and Gerald??

Aimee:

Maybe.

Junho:

I see. It's a love triangle then. I should warn you, I don't back down easily.

Aimee:

May the best swan duck whisperer win.

Twelve

"**Y**ou mean to say you watched a romantic sunset by the river by *yourself*?"

It's Thursday morning and Nikita and I are FaceTiming. I'm braiding my hair for the day, tying it into one long fishtail, while Nikita is sitting in her room, doing a face mask. We've been messaging since I got here, but we haven't been able to match up the time zones for a call until now. I've just finished updating her on everything I've been up to and, as I knew she would, she wanted to know everything about Junho, no details spared.

"I'm meeting him today, though," I say. "He invited me out to hang out with him and a couple friends who just came into town from Toronto. We're going to Seoul Forest."

Nikita leans back against the huge chicken plushie in her bed with a soft sigh. "I'm happy for you, Aims. You deserve a fun spring romance."

I flush, dropping my finished braid and reaching for my makeup pouch. "I never said romance. We're just hanging out."

"Yeah, I know. But it's written all over your face that you

like him. And you already have matching profile pictures, for goodness' sake. You know that's a couple thing?"

"You're ridiculous."

"I'm just saying, if you started dating, I wouldn't be mad about it."

"Yeah, because it would be so fun dating someone who might ditch you at any moment by disappearing into thin air," I say absent-mindedly, in the middle of putting on sunscreen.

Nikita pauses. I look up from my sunscreen bottle. "What?"

"You know you're great, right? Anyone would be lucky to date you if that's what you wanted."

I look back down at the sunscreen on my hands and quietly rub it into my face. I didn't mean to say that out loud. It's something that's crossed my mind a lot, especially after Russell asked me to the dance—what if I vanish in front of someone I like, in the middle of a date, in the middle of a kiss?—and it's no secret from Nikita that I've held dating at arm's length. But it feels awkward to talk about. I don't want to sound silly.

"No luck finding my mom yet," I say, changing the topic.

Nikita looks like she wants to say something more, but then bites her lip and follows my lead. "Sorry. I haven't been able to find anything about Baek Youngmi online either. She's nowhere."

"It's okay," I sigh. "It was a long shot. I really thought I was just going to walk into the old flower shop she worked at part-time like two decades ago or pedal around on a swan duck boat to find her, huh?"

"Maybe we need a new angle," Nikita says. "What's your grandparents' names again?"

"My grandparents? Why?"

"They owned the flower shop, right? I can't find your mom online, but maybe I can find something about them that'll lead us to your mom."

"I actually don't know what their names are. I've never met them and they're just Halmeoni and Harabeoji in my head." From what I can recall, Appa has never even spoken about my mom's parents to me, ever.

"Okay then. Remind me of the flower shop name?"

"Dream a Dream Flowers."

"I'll keep you updated on what I find," Nikita promises. "And Aims?"

"Yeah?"

She peels off her face mask, her skin bright and dewy underneath, and gives me a smile. "Have fun today."

Seoul Forest is an oasis in the middle of the city. Or at least, that's how Junho's friend Zack Im describes it to me. It's a huge park with walking trails and deer and a hot spot for outdoor concerts in warm weather, and it's Zack's favorite place in the city. "I come here every time I visit," he says.

Zack just came into Korea yesterday with his sister Bora and his boyfriend, Yul Park. He and Yul are only here for a week, cutting first-year university classes to join Bora, who's a year younger than me, on her spring break trip. They all have family in Seoul and seem to visit quite often, seeing how familiar they are with the city. I don't even need my subway app when I'm with them.

I meet them all at Wangsimni Station and am greeted by, "So *you're* Aimee! We've heard so much about you," from Yul, who promptly gets a nudge in the side from a pink-faced Junho. Junho smiles at me with a wave and I can't help but think of the tiny forget-me-not sprig now pressed into the pages of my journal, and the way we stayed up late last night chatting on KakaoTalk. Gomo even poked her head into my room to see why I was laughing so much by myself.

"Junho says you're from Vancouver," Yul says to me as we ride the subway, transferring to a line that'll take us to Seoul Forest. He's maybe the tallest guy I've ever met. I have to tilt my chin up to look at him. "I'm from there too. God, I miss the sushi. It's just not the same in the east."

I laugh. "That's what I hear. I applied to U of T, but my best friend is always trying to bribe me with sushi to stay in Vancouver instead."

"U of T! That's where Zack and I go. We'll show you around when you come."

"If I come," I say. "I might also end up in Kingston or Montreal."

Junho cocks his head to the side. "What do I have to bribe you with to choose Toronto instead?"

I bite back a smile, my cheeks warming again, and just shrug. "Name your offers."

Bora blows a strand of red-streaked hair out of her face. "When I graduate high school, I'm getting right out of Toronto. I'm going to London."

"London, Ontario?" Yul teases.

Bora rolls her eyes. "You're hilarious. England, obviously."

Zack nudges his sliding glasses up his nose. "I don't know if Umma will be very happy about you living in another country."

"Wae? She has you to take care of her. I want to see something new. Same as how Yul left Vancouver, and Aimee wants to come out east."

Is that why I want to go out east? To see something new? The thought makes me pause. I did only apply to schools in the east, but it's not because I'm bored of Vancouver or anything like that. I love Vancouver. But the idea of a fresh start, living on my own, away from Appa and the silence and the memories, appealed to me. Honestly, I feel a bit guilty thinking about leaving him on his own. Though I guess I've already started doing that, going on this trip without his permission.

"A different city isn't the same as a different country, though," Zack says. "It'll be a totally new and foreign culture. It'll take a while to adjust."

"Oppa, please, I can take care of myself," Bora says, scowling.

Yul and Junho exchange glances like they've heard this same conversation a million times. Junho smiles at me, including me in the exchange, and shrugs. "Siblings," he says.

"How's Minho doing?" I ask. I keep it general, unsure how much his friends know.

"Better, thanks. He's back at home, but still not talking to my mom. She doesn't know what to do with him." He sighs. "I had to try and talk both of them down yesterday."

"Do you have siblings, Aimee?" Bora asks.

I shake my head. Sometimes I wonder what it would have been like to have a sister or a brother, someone to fill the quiet between me and Appa.

"Only child, huh?" Yul says. "Lucky. I have four older siblings. Four! It's a crowd. And they're always looking down on me for being the short one."

Wow. If Yul is the short one, I can't imagine how tall the rest of his siblings must be.

We reach the Seoul Forest stop and get off the subway. I follow their lead out of the station and into the bright sunlight. The weather's been nice here, but still a bit chilly. I button up my black denim jacket, following the others toward the forest.

"So, Aimee, is there anything you want to do while you're in Korea?" Yul asks.

"Um . . ." Somehow, *find my mom so I can get some closure and stop disappearing* seems like a lot, so I just say, "I'm not sure. Do you have any recommendations?"

"Hmm, well, what do you like to do?"

"I like taking pictures."

"Namsan Tower has a nice view," Zack says.

"Great for couples!" Yul adds, putting an arm around Zack's shoulders. "Last time we came here together, we put a lock there with our names on it. We should go back and see if it's still there."

"Or," Bora says, her voice low and ominous, "you could go to Hapjeong Station and try and get a picture of the ghost."

I raise my eyebrows. "Ghost?"

Zack sighs. "Not this again."

"I saw it," Bora insists. "Last year when we came for the summer. And other people have seen it too. On the Hapjeong Station line two platform going toward Dangsan, there's a ghost that looks like a man with long black hair, just wandering around. He appears out of nowhere, crying, and then goes invisible again just like that." She snaps her fingers. "Lots of people have reported these brief sightings of him, but no one has actually caught him yet."

Huh. Interesting. I wonder if a ghost would even show up in a photograph. What if it's like one of those scary movies where you take a picture of nothing and then you take it to the darkroom and you see the ghost in the photo only after you develop it? I shudder. I'm not sure if I believe in ghosts myself, but if they do exist, I don't know if I would ever want to seek one out on purpose. Even for a potentially cool picture.

Yul shudders. "Creepy. Look, I have goose bumps." He holds out his arm.

"No, you don't," Zack says, rolling his eyes. "It's just a ghost story and we all know Bora is obsessed with ghost stories. Don't listen to her."

"Obsessed is a strong word," Bora says, indignant.

"Your favorite movie is *Casper* and you're literally wearing socks with ghosts on them right now."

"They're my Halloween socks!"

"It's March," Zack says flatly.

"Maybe I could make a webtoon about this," Junho says, his eyes lighting up. "*The Hapjeong Station Ghost*. That's a great title, isn't it?"

"Someone's already made a webtoon about it with that exact title," Bora says. "It's good, I've read it."

"Oh. Never mind then."

Bora looks thoughtful. "I just think the whole story is fascinating. You know some people say he's not a ghost at all, but a person stuck in a time loop? What's that condition again where that can happen?"

I freeze, my heart dropping at the sudden mention of time loops. Is she talking about . . . ?

"Sensory Time Warp Syndrome?" Junho suggests. I quickly turn to look at him, trying to gauge his expression. Does he know that I have it? His face is too neutral for me to tell.

"Yes, that!" Bora says. "There's a rumor that the ghost is actually just someone with STWS who's disappearing in and out of a memory. Like that Olympic snowboarder who went missing."

"That was never proven to be related to STWS, though," I say, trying to sound casual even though my whole body is tensing at the conversation. "We can't just assume that all strange things like that are because of STWS, right?"

"We can't assume that it's not either," Bora points out. "STWS is so mysterious and odd. Who *knows* how it works?"

"I'd hate to have a condition like that," Zack says, shaking his head. "It sounds so disruptive."

"Yeah, like imagine everyone thinking you're a ghost when really, you're just a human trapped in some kind of weird memory loop," Yul says. "That's kind of sad, isn't it?"

"Well, we can't rule out the possibility that he's actually a real ghost," Bora says. "Personally, that's still my theory."

My clothes suddenly feel itchy against my skin. Or maybe it's just me, uncomfortable everywhere. Should I tell them that I have STWS? But when would the appropriate time be? When they're comparing it to ghost stories or saying how awful it sounds to have this condition? It feels weird to say something, but it also feels weird to say nothing. I wish I could just run away from this entire conversation.

"You okay?" Junho asks quietly, tugging at my elbow.

His friends are still chatting, walking a few steps ahead of us. The topic has moved past STWS, but I'm still stuck in it. I'll always be stuck in it.

I look at Junho, trying to gauge again how much he knows. He looks worried, like he must see something on my face that shows I'm uncomfortable, but he doesn't have that knowing look in his eyes, the one that might hint that he gets the reason why.

"Yeah, totally okay," I say, giving him a reassuring smile. I don't want to spoil the day just because I'm being sensitive. He looks unconvinced.

Up ahead, Bora suddenly squeals, grabbing Zack's arm. "Oppa, look! A hodu gwaja stall! Let's get some."

"That girl loves red bean even more than she loves ghosts," Yul says, laughing as Bora drags Zack to the stall. "I swear, that's why she dyed her hair red. As an homage."

I hurry after them, avoiding any more questions from Junho. I try to gather myself and pull it together. Come on, Aimee. There's no reason to be so shook by this. Just put it behind you, like everyone else. Just have a good day.

I'm so lost in my thoughts that the smell from the hodu

gwaja stall hits me unguarded.

The scent is nutty and sweet, warm, walnuts and red bean, and I realize what's happening a breath before it happens. Too late to hide, too late to explain. Too late to do anything about it at all.

The last thing I see is Junho turning toward me, starting to ask a question, "Do you want to share . . . ?" And then I disappear.

Thirteen

Describe what it feels like to disappear in ten words or less.

It's something like this: ice-cold water on your face, harsh and sobering.

But instead of waking you up, it's a reminder that you could be in the middle of doing the most normal thing in the world, laughing with friends, but even so, you're not a normal person. You're gone.

I scramble to grab on to something in my mind, disoriented by the sudden bright light reflecting off the ocean in front of me. *What do you see?* Water rolling, sand sprawling, five-year-old me and my mom sitting on a beach towel with our noses in a brown paper bag. Memory Me is wearing a striped one-piece swimsuit, my mom in a big floppy sun hat and a white summer dress. Appa is standing ankle-deep in the ocean, pooling water in a plastic bucket. I recognize the place as Kitsilano Beach in Vancouver, but I don't recognize the memory.

"Umma, I want one!" Memory Me says, practically sticking her face inside the bag.

It jolts me, that word. Umma. I don't know when I went from thinking of her as "Umma" to just "my mom." After she left, Umma felt too intimate. Korean is a language I use mostly at home so it feels more personal even though I'm clumsier with it than English. "My mom" felt more fitting after there was no one at home to call Umma anymore.

What do you smell? My mom reaches into the bag and pulls out a hodu gwaja, a pastry round in shape like the walnut it's named after. The outside is soft and bready, the inside stuffed with red bean paste and chopped walnuts. It smells just like the one at the stall on the way to Seoul Forest. Not as fresh maybe, but with how closely Memory Me is smelling it, just as strong.

My mom passes one of the pastries to Memory Me and then picks one out for herself. The two of them cheers with their hodu gwaja. My mom is smiling as she takes a bite. I don't remember ever seeing her look so happy. Maybe because I was too busy at the time shoving the whole piece of hodu gwaja in my mouth.

That's probably why I also didn't notice that as my mom eats her pastry, her smile slowly fades, and tears begin to fill her eyes.

"Umma? What's wrong?" Memory Me asks, finally noticing.

My mom says nothing at first, only looks at the half-eaten hodu gwaja in her hand as silent tears well in her eyes. "It tastes like home," she says quietly to herself, and then she lets the tears fall.

Appa turns from the sea and notices her crying, stunned, starts running back, the bucket of water sloshing over the sides. "What happened? What's wrong?"

"Umma's hodu gwaja must taste bad," Memory Me says, concerned.

Appa's brow furrows. He kneels down next to my mom and takes her hand.

"Jib eh gago shipeo," she says.

"We can do that," Appa says. "We can go home right now. Aimee, pack your things."

"No." My mom shakes her head and repeats, "Jib eh gago shipeo. My real home."

I stare at the three of them—the three of us—and try to understand what's happening. I vaguely remember this day now, as much as I can remember something that happened when I was so young. I remember we found the fresh hodu gwaja for sale at H Mart, that my mom was so excited to find it that we bought a whole bag, brought it with us to the beach to snack on. She kept saying, "Neomu bangapda," which at the time I understood as, "It's so nice to see you."

But then we got to the beach. First she was so happy and now she's so sad. I stare at her as she lies back on the beach towel, covering her face with her hat and turning away from us. It almost looks as though she's curling into herself, arms tight around her body, protective.

"Is Umma sleeping?" Memory Me says, disappointed.

"She said she'd build sandcastles with me."

"Umma is tired," Appa says, smiling weakly. "How about we do the sandcastles together while she naps?"

And so they do. We do. I sit in the sand and watch Appa and Memory Me build their castle around my mom's blanket, like they're trying to protect her too, like she is the queen of the sand and we are taking her home.

I swallow the lump in my throat. Why do I have to come back to these memories? It wasn't so bad having STWS when the places I returned to were papier-mâché whales and hoddeok stalls with Junho. But why have all the ones from the past few years ended up with me here, watching my mom with no idea how I'm supposed to feel? If this is supposed to be some kind of sign of a greater purpose, I never asked for it.

I'm confused and sad and angry, even though I don't want to be. It feels selfish, but I can't help the pressure in my chest, burning, red, ruthless. I clench my fists, fingernails pressing into my palms. Why is *she* crying when she's the one who left me?

It's so hot, I'm sweating. The denim jacket that was perfect for March in Seoul is way too warm here. Everyone around me is wearing swimsuits, shorts, T-shirts. I peel off my jacket and walk away from myself, my mom, Appa. I can't go too far from them. They always have to be in my line of vision, otherwise I run into invisible walls that I can't go past, like the memory is contained in a box. But I don't have to look at them if I don't want to.

I stare out to the sea instead, trying to calm down. There are people on stand-up paddleboards on the water, a group of teenagers hollering at each other as they compete to see how far they can swim, and farther along the shoreline, a woman in a white coat staring out into the water, hands in her pockets.

She's totally overdressed for the weather, even more than me. From where I'm standing, I can't make out her face, her long dark hair blocking her features. *Who wears a coat like that in the summer?* I wonder.

"Hey, wait for me!" a voice yells as a teenage boy races for the water to join his friends. He's running straight toward the woman and I gasp, thinking there's going to be a collision. "Watch where you're going!" I want to shout, but I know he won't be able to hear me.

Only, he doesn't crash into the woman.

He goes straight through her, splashing into the water.

What do you feel? When I touch things in the memory state, it feels like solid air. When I press further, it feels like nothing at all. If something ever tried to touch me, it would just fall right through. Just like that boy walked through that woman like she wasn't even there.

What the hell? I blink and start to walk toward her. Slowly at first and then faster, kicking up the sand as I run.

"Hey!" I yell. "Hey!"

The woman startles. Did she hear me? How is that

possible? No one can hear me in the memories. Or at least, they're not supposed to. Not if they're part of the past. She starts to turn, but then suddenly, she's gone.

And then, before my foot can hit the sand again, so am I.

TOPIC: *Any advice for what to do when you come back from a memory?*

ProbablyEatingKettleCorn: Hi, RamenGuy. Thank you so much for your Standard Procedure List of Returning from the Past. It's definitely helped me deal with my disappearances and reappearances. Though I will say, the one part I'm still having trouble with is that last step of yours: EVERYTHING WILL BE ALL RIGHT. It's hard for me to really believe that when I return from a memory. I just don't know how to explain myself, especially when other people see me appear out of thin air. I wish I didn't care so much, but ugh. Why is it so hard to be chill?

IchirakuRamenGuy33: Don't feel bad. That's the hardest step. Also, official petition to rename this forum "Why Is It So Hard to Be Chill?"

Fourteen

AND THEN JUST LIKE THAT.

Four pairs of eyes stare at me, five counting the ajumma at the hodu gwaja stall. Bora's mouth drops open. "You—what—what was that?"

"Oh shit," Zack says, realization dawning on his face. "You have Sensory Time Warp Syndrome."

My head pounds, dizzy. "Hey, hey, give her some space," Junho says, shooting his friends a look. He steps toward me, expression softening. "Are you okay?"

I nod, even though I feel very not okay; in fact, the exact opposite of okay. "I'm fine," I say. I really mean I'm FINE. I wish Nikita was here. I wish no one was here. "What time is it?"

HOW LONG WAS I GONE FOR?

"Time? It's 11:47 a.m.," Junho says.

I look at my phone, screen frozen to 11:40 a.m. I was only gone for seven minutes. Not long. Not short.

"We thought you were pulling a joke on us at first," Yul says, his voice full of shock. "Like hide-and-seek or something. We were about to go looking for you!"

"Ajumma swore she saw you disappear, but we didn't believe her," Bora adds, glancing at the woman behind the hodu gwaja stall staring at me with wide saucer eyes. "I can't believe that happened. We were just talking about STWS too . . ."

The ajumma at the stall isn't the only one staring at me. Lots of strangers passing by on the street who saw me reappear have stopped to gawk, some even with their phone cameras out, trained in my direction like they're waiting for me to disappear again, like it's some kind of party trick. I feel like I'm back at the art show, head throbbing, people asking if I can do it one more time so they can catch it on video.

I feel sick.

WHAT NOW?

"Aimee?" Junho's voice feels like it's coming from a million miles away. It's hard to breathe. There are so many people. It feels like my brain is trying to process too much at once and it's short-circuiting, unsure where to land, so it just keeps spiraling, down down down.

Everyone is staring.

My mom curled up on a beach towel.

Don't look at me.

Sandcastle walls around her.

I need to get out of here.

The person staring out into the sea. Who was that? What were they doing in my memory?

I can't breathe.

"Aimee?" Junho says again.

It's too much.

EVERYTHING WILL BE ALL RIGHT.

Nothing is okay, but I tell Junho it is. I even try to smile. He doesn't believe me, but it doesn't matter. The only thing that matters right now is getting the hell out of here.

"I actually have to get going now," I say. I try to sound normal. I fail. "I forgot there's something I need to do today."

The others exchange glances. I hate that they do that.

"I'll go with you," Junho says.

"No, no, please, don't let me ruin Seoul Forest. Go without me. I'll check it out another time."

Before they can protest, I'm already walking away, waving, smiling, cheeks hurting. Junho takes a step forward like he wants to follow me, but I don't give him a chance. I turn my back on him and the others and run for the station, dropping my smile.

I get out of there as fast as I can.

Junho:

Hey, lmk when you get home. And if you want to talk.

Junho:

Hope you're ok.

Me:

> Home now! Thanks! Going to rest up now but will talk to you soon!

There we go. The use of exclamation marks in my text should show Junho that I'm definitely fine. Or just unhinged.

He and his friends will probably never want to see me again.

I'm back at Gomo's house, in my pajamas, curled up in bed. It's only 1:00 p.m., but there's nowhere else I'd rather be right now than here. Alone, blinds drawn, blocking out the light.

I can't stop thinking about the memory. About the person I saw there who looked like they didn't belong. Who definitely didn't belong.

"The boy ran right through her," I whisper to myself. "She was wearing a white coat in a memory of summer."

I lie like that for a long time, not moving, just replaying the moment over and over in my head. An hour passes. Two. It's 3:00 p.m. for me, 11:00 p.m. in Vancouver when my phone pings with a text from Nikita.

Nikita:

> Hey! Let me know if you're around to talk, I think I might have a new lead for you.

I stare at my phone. Normally, I'd be curious and call

her back right away, but right now I just feel numb.

There's only one person I want to talk to right now.

I get up from bed and open the blinds, squinting from the sudden light filling the room. I FaceTime Appa, waiting for him to pick up. His face appears after the second ring. I see him sitting at our kitchen table, cereal box and green mug already set out for the next morning. It's strangely comforting in a way that makes me want to cry.

"Aimee? Is everything okay?" he says.

At first, I think he must be able to tell from my face that something is wrong. And then I realize it's probably because I rarely FaceTime him. It would be unusual for me to call him just to chat on a regular day, but lately, with things so weird between us? It must be extra alarming.

"Yeah, everything's fine," I say.

"Okay. That's good. How's your aunt?"

"She's great. We went to go eat ddeokbokki at the shijang the other day."

A faint smile crosses his lips. "I used to eat that a lot."

I want him to tell me more, but he doesn't. I want to ask him if he remembers that day at the beach when we built a sandcastle around my mom, if he still thinks about the way she wept over a walnut pastry, how he felt when she did, if he knows whether or not she had STWS and maybe even if he knows whether or not that person in the memory who vanished before me was her because I can't shake the possibility that it might have been.

But the silence between us grows too long, too awkward, and before I can figure out the words to say anything I want to, he says, "I should probably get ready for bed now. Tell your aunt I say hi, okay?"

I swallow all my questions. "Okay," I reply because there is nothing else to say. "Have a good sleep."

He smiles and waves and then we hang up.

Gomo comes home to find me in bed again. She cracks open the bedroom door, peering inside. "Aimee? Are you in here?"

"Mmm?" I say, voice muffled by pillows. I lift my head. "I'm here."

"Ja?"

"No, I'm not sleeping. Just resting."

She comes in, lays a hand on my forehead. "Are you sick?"

I shake my head. She looks at the blinds, closed again after my call with Appa.

"It's a bit stuffy in here," she says. "I'll open a window."

I let her. I don't realize how stuffy it was until I feel the breeze. Gomo takes a long, careful look at me and then claps her hands together. "You know what I'm craving for dinner tonight? Kimchi sujebi. Will you come out and help me make it?"

I'm not very hungry, but I don't want to be rude so I just

nod. I muster up all the strength I have and lug myself out of bed. My whole body feels heavy.

Gomo has me wash my hands and make the dough. Sujebi is a hand-torn noodle soup, so I'm doing the noodle part while she gets to work on the broth.

It took a lot of mental energy to get to the kitchen, but once I start working with my hands, I feel a little better, a little lighter. Gomo sings a Korean ballad while she works, reminding me of the time she came to stay with us when I was a kid. By the time I tear the big ball of dough I made into smaller pieces for the soup, I'm humming along.

"Jal meokgetseumnida," I say as we sit at the table with our bowls of sujebi. The kimchi broth is a deep orange, with rectangles of kelp topping the hand-torn pieces of dough. I dip my spoon into the soup and eat. It's spicy and refreshing and, I realize, exactly what I needed.

"How is it? Is the salt level okay?" Gomo asks.

"It's perfect."

She beams. "Good."

"I talked to Appa earlier today. He says hi."

"Oh, that's nice! I've been sending him regular updates since you got here. It's good that you talked to him."

Interesting. Why would Appa ask me how Gomo is doing if he's been keeping in touch with her himself? Do we have so little to talk about that he's asking me questions now that he already knows the answers to?

"What's wrong?" Gomo asks.

"Hmm?"

"You're making this face." Gomo scrunches her forehead in a concerned manner. I try to relax, touching my fingers to my own forehead.

"It's nothing. It's just . . . sometimes I don't know how to talk to Appa."

She nods, understanding. "I know. He has trouble with his words."

"Yeah." I eat my sujebi, quiet. And then I say, "I disappeared today outside a hodu gwaja stall."

Gomo's eyes widen. "Did you? Are you okay? That must have been shocking to have it happen in a foreign country."

"It was kind of, yeah." Her response makes me feel more open, so I continue. "I want to see a specialist about it, but Appa won't let me. I don't know why he's so stubborn about it. He won't even listen when I bring it up."

"A specialist?"

"Yeah, like a therapist or psychologist who specializes in Sensory Time Warp Syndrome."

Gomo pauses, taking a bite of sujebi and chewing thoughtfully. "Well, your dad's spent a long time in Canada, but he still has a very traditional Korean mindset in some ways," she says finally. "Things like seeing a therapist are still frowned upon by some here. People would rather hide that they're struggling than show others they have a problem, and they think everyone should do the same. Not everyone is like that, of course, and maybe things are changing slowly, but stigmas are strong here, and your dad is coming from a different place. He's just trying to protect you in the ways he knows how."

I've never thought of that, how Appa's resistance to me seeking professional help might be rooted in cultural reasons and that he might be coming from a protective place. I've always just felt like he was disregarding me and everything I had to say because it made him uncomfortable.

"That might be true, but I would feel a lot less lonely if he would listen to where I'm coming from too," I say with a sigh.

She reaches across the table and pats my hand. "That is fair."

After we eat, Gomo tells me to wait in the living room. She disappears into her bedroom and comes out a moment later, holding a photo album.

"I dug this out of my closet. I thought you might be interested in looking at it." She sits next to me on the couch, opening the album on my lap. The first photo is of a little girl holding a baby in her arms and sticking her tongue out at the camera. They're at a park that looks familiar, a huge garden sprawling in the background behind them.

"Who's that?" I ask.

"Me and your dad," Gomo says. "I'm seven years older

than him so I treated him like my own personal doll when he was first born." She chuckles.

I look closer at the photo. "Isn't this Queen Elizabeth Park in Vancouver?"

"Yep! We moved to Canada just before your dad was born. He spent the first couple years of his life there, and then we moved back to Korea after our mom fell ill. She wanted to receive treatment in a language she understood and be in her hometown." She flips a page, looking wistfully at a family photo with her parents. "It's too bad you never got to meet your grandparents. They would have loved you."

I look at the photo too, touching the page lightly with my fingertips. I knew Appa was born in Canada, which affected his decision to immigrate there again later, and that his parents passed away early—his mom when he was a teenager and his dad shortly before I was born—but I've never seen many photos of this time in his life. We hardly have any back home.

Gomo's phone rings and she glances at the caller ID. "Oh, it's a friend of mine. You keep looking, I'll be right back." She gets up and disappears into her room to answer, leaving me with the album.

I flip through slowly, savoring each photo, pausing on some to take a snapshot on my phone. There's even one of Appa as a middle schooler, squished between Gomo and a teenage boy who has to be Mr. Kim. He has the exact same face, though he had a full head of hair then. Their names are written in three different styles of handwriting across the photo: *ROH MISU, ROH HYUNWOO, KIM SUNGMIN*. Each of them must have signed their own name on the photo. I smile, taking a quick picture of that one, and turn the page.

A photo of Appa and my mom looks back at me and my breath catches in my throat. They're young, teenagers sitting on a swing set, looking at each other and laughing. They seem so happy. So in love.

There are more of them when they were younger, in their school uniforms. I get a glimpse of the Appa who Mr. Kim and Gomo keep telling me about, the one who talked too much and lived to make my mother laugh. His smile is bright and open in every photo. And my mom, well, she's beautiful. Even at that age, she has the kind of eyes that you can't help but fall into.

In one of her teen pictures, she's holding a camera up to her face, a classic photo of someone taking a photo. I look closer. It's not just any camera, it's *my* camera. I always knew it once belonged to her, but it's strange seeing it in her hands. I wonder if she left it behind on purpose with the hopes that I'd pick it up one day. The thought makes me feel close to her, but knowing that I might never know the answer makes me feel farther away again.

I flip the page. It's another one of Appa and my mom, but this one looks more recent. It was definitely taken in

Vancouver after they immigrated. Maybe Appa sent it to Gomo or she printed it out for the album herself. They are both smiling at the camera, Appa's arm around my mom's shoulders, but their smiles are noticeably different from the other pictures. A little less bright, a little less open. In the photo next to that one, I'm there too, a small little toddler in overalls.

But the thing that makes me stop and stare?

My mom, hair long and dark, swept over one shoulder, wearing a white coat that drops down to her knees.

Exactly like the one I saw on the person in my memory.

THINGS I DON'T KNOW

- Can you see other time travelers in your memories?

- Who is the woman in the white coat?

- What if it was my mom?

- Am I losing my mind?

Fifteen

Could it be her?

I stay up all night wondering.

I don't know how it's possible. I've never seen anyone in my memory visits before who wasn't supposed to be there, so I feel like my mind is jumping to wild conclusions. I'm reaching. I know I am.

But what if I'm not?

What if it really is her?

I scour the STWS forums for answers, but there isn't as much discussion as I hoped there would be on seeing out-of-place people in your memories. There is, however, a reminder about the STWS meetup happening this Saturday.

Talking to Gomo today made me realize just how lonely I am. It feels like such a strange thing to say when I'm surrounded by kind people. The sujebi in my belly and the forget-me-not in my journal are just two small examples of that. I could call Nikita at any time and I know she would answer. Even now, my phone is pinging with texts from her, asking if I'm free to talk. And as distant as Appa is, I know Gomo's right when she says he's coming from a place where he cares. It feels almost ungrateful to be lonely when I have all of this in my life.

So I keep it to myself—that heavy feeling that at the end of the day, when I disappear, I disappear alone—because I don't want to be a burden with my heaviness when it feels as though I shouldn't be heavy at all, that all the good in my life should outweigh the bad.

What do I really have to complain about?

Why do I feel so sad?

I stare at the meetup information on my phone. It could help. Meeting other people with STWS. Even reading comments online makes me feel less alone. Maybe going to this meeting and talking to strangers in person is a leap I need to take.

The image of the woman in the white coat standing at the water comes back to me again. And I can't help but think, she might understand. If anyone in the world, she might.

I turn off the light, crawl into bed. I came to Korea to find answers, but all I've found so far are more questions.

A plan slowly begins to form in my head as I drift off to sleep.

Tomorrow.

Tomorrow I will find some answers.

Friday morning, I head back toward Seoul Forest.

I've never tried to go back to the past on purpose before. I don't tell anyone about it. Not Gomo, or even Nikita, whose texts I still haven't answered. It feels almost shameful, like I'm doing something I definitely shouldn't be doing. And maybe I am. Maybe after all my talk about how I want to stop disappearing, I'm contradicting myself by doing the exact opposite now.

But I have to know. I have to see her again.

I retrace my steps from yesterday, getting off at the station, exiting, walking down the street toward the hodu gwaja stall. I see it right away. I wear sunglasses and a hat pulled low over my face, just in case the ajumma at the stall recognizes me and makes a big deal out of me vanishing right in front of her yesterday.

As I approach the stall, I take a deep breath. Sweet walnuts and red bean.

But. I'm still here.

I take another deep inhale. The smell is strong, but around me, people keep on strolling down the sidewalk, the ajumma keeps on flipping hodu gwaja, and I am definitely still in Seoul and not at Kitsilano Beach.

Okay. So now that I actually want to disappear, apparently that's not how it works.

"Can I help you?" the ajumma at the stall asks, peering at me over her pan.

"Oh, uh, sorry." I realize I've just been standing there, smelling the air like some kind of weirdo. At least she doesn't recognize me. "I'll take one bag, please."

I pay and hurry away.

This time, I actually make it all the way to Seoul Forest. Did Junho, Bora, Zack, and Yul have a good time yesterday? I wonder what they all think of me now. What Junho will think of me now.

The park is exactly as Zack described it. Lush and vibrant and calm. I walk along the trails, pausing to take photos of the many flowers blooming in the grass, clutching my bag of hodu gwaja. All the while, I think of a new plan, eventually taking a seat on a bench in an empty, quiet area.

I open the bag of walnut cakes. It didn't work the way I thought it would, but maybe if I try to focus more. I take one out and hold it in my palms like a tiny bird's egg, delicate, cautious, lifting it close to my nose. I close my eyes and inhale, picturing the beach in my mind.

Sandcastles and red bean.

Her floppy hat.

Walnuts and the person by the sea, staring out.

I hear ocean waves. At first, I think I must be imagining it, but then I slowly open my eyes, and—I can't believe it. I did it.

Describe what it feels like to disappear in ten words or less: familiar, as if the memory is saying, "Welcome back."

The usual falling feeling isn't there this time. It's different when you choose to go. And maybe because I've been here before, just recently, it's not as disorienting as it usually is. I take in the same details: Memory Me in her striped swimsuit, my mom with the hodu gwaja, the two of them clinking their cakes together like they're champagne glasses. She takes a bite; her eyes fill with tears. Appa runs over.

"Umma's hodu gwaja must taste bad," Memory Me says.

This time, I don't continue watching. This time, I look to the water. I scour the shoreline for the person in white, but she's not there. Everything else is exactly the same: the people on the paddleboards, the teenagers in the water, the boy running to join his friends. But no woman watching over it all.

I wait. And wait. My eyes bore holes into the sand where she stood. But no one comes.

Disappointment fills me. I sit down on the sand, the hodu gwaja still in my hands. So much for that. But I guess I did confirm one thing.

Whoever I saw yesterday wasn't part of the original memory. She doesn't belong here.

So then who was she? And why was she in my memories?

"Look, Aimee, I made a turtle," Appa says to Memory Me, pointing to a sand turtle guarding the castle. "You can name him."

My attention drifts back to their direction. I look at the easy way Appa smiles at the sand turtle, crafted by his hands. A little lopsided but a turtle nevertheless. And then I think of his face on my phone screen the other day as we FaceTimed, the awkward silences between us, the unsaid words, the distance. I try to imagine the Appa of now making turtles in the sand and it's difficult. I can't.

"I want to name him Alex!" Memory Me shouts. She grabs the empty plastic bucket with one hand and Appa's with the other, dragging him back toward the sea. "Let's make more sand turtles. More!"

My chest aches. How is he the same person? How am I?

FROM THE PAGES OF AIMEE'S JOURNAL: ART SPREAD

The paper is covered in stickers from Blue Bunny Bakery. There are ten of them. In writing at the bottom: *Appa has been taking me to the bakery to collect all the stickers! I think he is tired of the bread there. Two more to go!*

Last two stickers unfound.

Sixteen

I spend the rest of the day at Seoul Forest. I take photos to ground myself again after the memory visit, to remind me that I'm here now, in my own world. I take so many the battery in my Canon dies and I switch over to my phone, but it doesn't quite have the same effect. The weight of it is missing. I go home.

As I approach Gomo's apartment, I see a familiar figure at the outdoor gym right outside. I've noticed these gyms all over Seoul, almost like a playground except instead of swings and slides there are ellipticals and weights. Not as fancy as what you might find in an indoor gym, but functional nevertheless. Mostly, I see elderly folks using these machines. I get closer. Swinging his legs on one of those ellipticals is none other than Junho.

We see each other at the same time. My stomach swoops at the sight of him.

"Aimee!" he yells, raising his hand in the air. A look of alarm crosses his face as he loses his balance and nearly falls off the elliptical.

"Whoa." I jog over. "Careful, sir, you don't want to

break your back."

He laughs, steadying himself. "I'm clumsy, not a hundred years old."

"You sure? Because from where I was standing, I think you should get lessons from the grandmas and grandpas at the park before you hurt yourself. They'll show you how it's done."

He grins and hops off the machine to stand in front of me. "One day, I'll be an Olympic-level athlete on that thing. Just you wait."

There's a beat of silence and the air between us gets awkward. I take a step back, rubbing my arms. "So what brings you here?"

"My dad is visiting your aunt," he says, gesturing toward the apartment. "And I thought I'd wait out here for . . . the . . . uh, sunset."

"Sunset?" I raise my eyebrows and look up at the sky, still blue. "That'll be a while."

"Right." He smiles, tentative. "Well, I guess while I was waiting for the sunset, I was also maybe waiting for you. I wanted to see if you're doing okay."

My guard goes up at the same time my heart grows soft. He's worried about me. I'm torn between telling him everything is okay and telling him the truth. That I've been lonely and confused and I feel like I'm losing my mind, that I have theories, that they might sound strange, but they might be real and I don't know where that leaves me.

"I'm okay," I say at last. "Thanks for asking."

"Are you sure?" he says, insistent. "Because if there's a problem with you, I can help fix it."

I take a step back at that, my guard rising higher. "I don't really need fixing."

"Shit. I phrased that wrong. I didn't mean it like *you* need fixing," he says quickly, backtracking. "It's just yesterday, you seemed so distressed by what happened and I wanted to follow you, but I wasn't sure if that's what you wanted. I mean, we don't know each other very well yet, and I feel like me and my friends didn't make things any easier for you either. We all feel terrible for how we were talking about STWS without knowing you had it right before you disappeared. That must have made you feel so weird. I want to apologize for that, and they all want to say sorry too. Also, there were so many strangers just staring at you, and I wish I just told everyone to get lost and . . . and . . ."

I stare at him. He trails off, staring down at his feet. "And I'm sorry. I'm rambling. I'm usually better at this."

"Better at what?"

"Better at making things better." He takes a breath. "What I really wanted to say is: If you wanted to talk, I'll listen."

My defenses lower. Something he said in his rambling echoes in my mind. We don't know each other very well *yet*, he said. Yet. I could keep holding him at a distance because we're still new to each other. I could thank him politely for checking in, and then say goodbye. Or I could take a step in, open up. He's not scared off by my disappearing. There's still time for us to get to know each other better if I let us.

"As you saw, I have Sensory Time Warp Syndrome," I say. "Did you know I have it?"

"No. If my dad knows, he never mentioned it."

"Ah." There's the confirmation, though the surprise on his face yesterday probably said it all. I press on. "My trigger sense is smell, so sometimes when I smell things linked to a memory, I go back to that memory for a while. That's what happened yesterday."

He nods slowly like he's absorbing what I'm saying. "That's what we thought. Though we weren't totally sure what caused it. Was it the hodu gwaja?"

"Yeah."

I brace myself for questions. Not that I mind questions. If anything, I appreciate them, especially if they come from people who care about me. But like Junho said, we don't know each other very well yet. I have no idea what he'll say and I don't want him to think that I need to be fixed.

He shakes his head. "Those walnuts are dangerous. You can never trust them. I choked on one once as a kid, you know."

"Seriously?"

"Oh yeah. My brother had to come to my rescue. He said he saved my life that day."

I laugh and he raises an eyebrow.

"You find my near-death experience hilarious, do you?"

"Only because you're still standing, very much alive. If the walnut took you out, I would definitely not be laughing." I make my face look solemn.

"Good. Because if the walnut *did* take me out, you'd be in charge of avenging me."

"Me? Why me?"

"Because I wrote it in my final will and testament. Those are binding."

I laugh again, not able to hold a straight face. "How would I be in your will if the walnut killed you as a kid? Would you travel back in time to write it or something?"

The words slip out without me even thinking. They hang between us for a moment, but before it can get awkward, Junho fills the space, tentative curiosity in his eyes. "Can you? I mean, travel back in time and change things? I heard that that's not how STWS works, but . . ."

"You're right." I shake my head. "It's not how it works. I can't change anything, I can only watch."

"Is it scary?" he asks.

"Sometimes," I admit. "It's super disorienting. It always takes me a minute to figure out where I am. And when the memories are . . . difficult to be in, it's hard being stuck there until it's over." I look away, staring at the exercise machines as I continue. "But sometimes the memories are nice and it feels good to visit."

Like you and me at the hoddeok stand, I add silently

to myself. It was one of the first memories I went back to when I started disappearing. Junho's seven-year-old arms were covered in drawings, a map of ink etched into his skin. Robots and monkeys and walruses in top hats. The drawings on his right arm were much steadier than the ones on his left because he was left-handed.

"I want one too," I said, holding out my arm.

He looked at me, all big brown eyes. "What do you want?"

I thought for a moment. My mom had been gone for a year at that point. I was still young enough to believe she might come back. "I want a pear."

"A pear?"

"It's my favorite fruit." It had been hers too.

"Like a big Korean pear or one of those green pears you see in Canadian grocery stores?"

"Korean."

"Okay."

He drew, his fingers sticky on my wrist from the sweet pancake. It smelled like cinnamon and honey. He drew the pear, added flowers to the background, taking care on every detail. I decided then that I liked him very much.

The Junho in front of me now has no pretend tattoos on his arms, but his fingers are still stained with ink from drawing. I don't know if he remembers our shared memory, so I keep it to myself.

"Was the memory you went to yesterday a nice one or

a difficult one?" he asks.

I pause for a long time. He's already worried about me. I don't want him to worry more. But we've come this far in our conversation; I don't want to start pretending now either. "It was difficult."

He thinks for a moment and then he holds out his hand. "Come on."

I blink. "Where?"

"To relieve some stress." I take his hand. I wonder if he feels the way sparks fly across my palm when his skin touches mine. I wonder if he feels it too. He grins, leading me to the two side-by-side ellipticals. "I challenge you to a race."

There's a question mark in my laugh as I climb onto one of the machines, regretfully letting go of his hand, already missing the feel of it. I decide to follow his lead and see where this takes me. "How do we race on ellipticals that don't move?"

"We'll just have to observe how fast our legs go. It'll be a thirty-second sprint. I won't be easy on you, so you better go as fast as you can."

"For some reason, I'm not worried."

"Ouch. You'll regret those words, Aimee Roh. Ready?"

"Ready."

"Go!"

We race, legs pumping, arms pushing. I go so hard my heart rate picks up right away and I'm sweating already.

Twenty-seven seconds. Twenty-eight. Twenty-nine. Thirty.

We stop, wheezing. "Who won?" he asks.

"You weren't keeping track?"

He laughs, loud, and then turns to me, out of breath, cheeks red. He stares for so long that I can feel my face flush even more than from the exercise.

"What I wanted to say earlier, before I messed it up. It's more like this. I can't possibly understand what it's like for you to disappear without any warning," he says, his face serious now. "I think something like that might make me feel like I'm walking between two worlds or something. Always on the edge, about to tip over. But whenever you need a reminder of what's real, well, I'm here for you." He smiles. "That's all."

Here for you. It's such a present term. *Here.* I take his words, hold them close, feel their heartbeat. It makes my chest ache with the gift of it and I don't take it for granted.

I lean against the elliptical. "Actually, I think my legs were moving slightly faster than yours."

"The judges demand proof."

"Rematch?"

"You're on."

Snapshot: the boy with the ink-stained fingers, the girl who walks on the edge of the world, they race without moving an inch. Their legs are a blur, that's how fast they're going, or at least that's how fast they think they're going. It doesn't matter. What matters is they're here.

* * *

That night, hair up in a towel after taking a shower, I sit in bed and FaceTime Nikita. It'll be early in the morning for her, but I know she'll be awake.

Just as I expected, she appears on my phone screen after two rings, yelling, "Aims! Where've you been? Didn't you see my texts? I know you're on vacation and time zones and whatever, but I've been dying to talk to you!"

"Sorry, sorry," I say. Normally, I would leave it at just that, but tonight I'm feeling more open. "I had another disappearance yesterday and haven't been in a great place. It was hard to reply your messages, but I saw them all. And I made replies in my head so we can talk about it now."

As open as I'm feeling, it's still hard to get the words out. Nikita's face softens. "Oh damn. Another disappearance, huh? How are you feeling?"

"Better today. Fine, even."

"Fine or FINE?"

I smile. "Lowercase."

She surveys my face for a second like she's not sure if she should believe me, but then she smiles back. "Okay. Well that's good to hear. You do look happy."

"Yeah? I feel happy," I say.

And lighter too, I think. I came to Korea to look for my mom, and while I'm barely any closer to that, I'm beginning to feel like maybe it's okay if I don't find her. Not just because it was a long shot from the start, but because it feels like there's a different way to find peace now. A way that involves being *here* with the people who are already in front of me.

And then Nikita says, "So do you want to hear about my new lead?"

I hesitate. I've been so caught up the past two days in looking for my mom in my memories that I kind of forgot about looking for her right here in Korea. It wouldn't be the hardest thing to just let go of the whole investigation and spend the rest of my time here having fun with Junho and Gomo.

But I've come this far. Would it hurt to at least hear what Nikita has to say?

"Go ahead," I say.

"First, I want you to say, 'Nikita Lai-Sanders is a master detective.'"

"Shouldn't I technically say that *after* you share the information?"

"Fine. Okay, look at your phone. I just sent you a link."

A text pops up on my screen. I press it and it leads me to the website for a flower shop in Gwangju called It's a Good Flower Day. "What is this?" I ask. "And how did you read it? The website is entirely in Korean."

"Google Translate is my friend," Nikita's voice says, her video paused as I scroll through the website. "A somewhat unreliable, inaccurate friend, but it gives me the gist. Also, Mary Lee from student council may have received a lot of annoying texts from me this week asking translation questions, but never mind. Look at the 'about' section."

I do. A photo of an elderly couple in front of the shop appears.

"Are you reading? I can't see your face."

"I'm reading," I say.

The paragraph below the photo reads: *Hello, we are the flower shop owners Baek Woojin and Shin Chansung. We have a long history of working in flower markets and even operated a popular flower shop in Seoul for fifteen years. Eventually, we decided to move back to our hometown in Gwangju, where we are now the proud owners of It's a Good Flower Day. Please come visit us and our flowers!*

Below that, there's a map showing the location of the flower shop. I zoom into the photo, looking closer at their faces. Up close, there's a familiarity to them even though I've never seen them before in real life, and suddenly I realize. Chills run up my spine.

"Are you still there?" Nikita says.

I tap back into our video chat and she's looking at me, expectant and eager.

"Are these my grandparents?" I say, my voice hushed.

Baek Woojin. Shin Chansung. Women in Korea don't change their last name after they get married, but the grandfather in the photo is a Baek, just like my mom, and the family resemblance in their features is uncanny. Too uncanny to be a coincidence.

"That's what I was going to ask you!" Nikita says. "I dug way back on all of Dream a Dream Flowers' online activity and found a super old review from someone saying, 'We'll miss you in Seoul but best of luck in Gwangju!' So it got me thinking, maybe after your grandparents sold the shop in Seoul, they opened another one in Gwangju. I did a deep-dive search for flower shops in the city of Gwangju and this is the only one I found owned by a couple that could be your grandparents' age, and the man's last name is the same as your mom's. Am I reaching or do we have something here?"

I stare at her. "Nikita Lai-Sanders, you are a master detective."

She blows kisses at the screen. "Thank you, thank you."

"I can't believe you went to such lengths to find this."

"What? Of course. You're my best friend and I know how much this means to you. I have no idea where Gwangju is, but maybe you can visit them or even call?"

Between my failed memory trip to the beach this morning and Junho and Nikita showing up for me afterward, I'm feeling seriously emotional. "Honestly, thank you. You're unbelievable."

"If you really want to thank me, you can buy Mary Lee lunch for a week when you're back. I owe her big-time," she says. There's a pinging sound from her end and she looks at her screen, distracted.

"What's that?" I ask.

"Oh, I just got a text. It's, uh, David."

"Your ex? He's still texting you?"

"Yeah . . ." Her voice trails off and she looks at the ceiling, away from me.

I pause, taking a closer look at her. "Wait. Are you wearing a knit sweater?"

"So? It's cold today."

"You're Eternal Summer Nikita. You never wear cold-weather clothes. The only time I've seen you wear a sweater is when your dog Orlando died and that time you lost the race for class rep."

She picks at a loose thread on her sweater, twirling it around her finger.

"Nik? What's going on?"

"Well. To be honest, my parents told me that they're planning on moving to Taiwan after I start at UBC in September," she says. "My grandma's not doing so well and my mom wants to be close to her."

"Oh." I lean against the big pillows on my bed, sighing deeply. "I'm sorry to hear that about your grandma."

"Thanks. I'm scared for her. But honestly—and this is going to sound really selfish—right now I'm more sad that my parents are leaving. I mean, I have amazing grades. More extracurriculars than anyone in our grade. I feel like I could have gone to school anywhere. But UBC has a good international relations program and I thought staying in Vancouver would be nice to be close to family. I'm not saying they're the only reason I chose this school, but they were a big reason. And now they're not even going to be here. And neither are you come September."

The thread snaps in her finger and she brushes it away, letting it fly off in the air. Her voice gets quiet. "I know I'm being a baby about it. I'm graduating high school soon, for god's sake! It's just, I'm going to miss them. And I'm going to miss you. You being gone this spring break hit me that soon, this is going to be our norm. FaceTimes. Time differences."

"Only three hours," I offer, even though I know that's not the point.

"I know. I just feel like everyone is leaving me behind, which is totally ridiculous, but I can't help it." She sighs. "Everyone except David anyway. He'll be here, going to SFU in September. So we've kind of been texting and hooking up here and there. I know, I know! We broke up because he's the worst. He talks over me all the time and he doesn't shower nearly as much as he should. I've just been a little . . . lonely, I guess."

Her voice gets even smaller and I wish I could reach through the screen and wrap her in a hug. "Nik, why didn't you tell me?" I ask. All this time, we've just been talking about me. In my loneliness, I never imagined that Nikita was feeling lonely too.

"You've just been going through so much lately," she says. "And how can I complain to you when you're going through such bigger things? I feel like my problems aren't even problems."

"Hey, don't compare," I say. Tears spring up in my eyes despite myself. "Loneliness is loneliness. One person's experience doesn't wipe away another's."

"Oh my god, are you crying?" Tears fill her own eyes. "Why are you crying?"

"I don't know. Why are you?"

"I don't know!"

We're both laughing now and still crying at the same time. I wipe my eyes with the back of my hand. "I'm sorry I haven't even asked lately how you're doing."

"It's okay. It feels good to talk about it now." She grabs a Kleenex and blows her nose.

"We should do that more," I say. "Talk about things."

"Deal. But first let me change out of this ugly-ass sweater."

I laugh and she does, and then, for the first time in a long while, we talk for hours, not worrying about being a burden, not worrying about anything at all.

REASONS NOT TO GIVE UP LOOKING FOR MY MOM

- Nikita found a new lead about my grandparents. My grandparents who I've never met before but could potentially meet now.
- None of my questions have been answered yet about why she left and whether or not she has STWS.
- I might have seen her in my memory.
- She might still be the person who understands me the most.
- Maybe there are different ways to find closure, but I need to see this through until the end.
- I need to know.

Seventeen

The Seoul STWS meetup is happening today, Saturday afternoon at an Ediya Coffee branch, and I've decided to go.

After yesterday's conversation with Nikita, I'm feeling a fresh resolve to focus on why I came to Korea in the first place: to find answers about my mom. Today at this meetup, I'm going to figure out if the lady in the white coat was her, if it's even possible for her to appear in my memories like that. If I can ask anyone my questions, I'm hoping it will be the people at this meetup.

I take forever deciding what to wear, eventually landing on a linen white jumpsuit with mustard-yellow clay earrings. A comfort outfit to give me strength. But by the time I get to the café, I don't know where all my courage goes. I hover outside the door, second-guessing.

Maybe I should leave.

Maybe there will be another exploitative person there, like at the Vancouver meetup.

Maybe it makes more sense to start by posting on the forums first. You can't say you're meeting online friends if you're not even friends online.

Maybe—

"Excuse me, are you here for the STWS meeting?" a voice behind me says.

I jump, slowly turning around to see a girl in a ponytail and round glasses. I assume by the Korea University varsity jacket she's wearing that she's a student there.

"Um, yes," I reply.

She adjusts the backpack hanging off her shoulder and holds out her hand. "Nice to meet you. I'm Yoo Seri."

"Roh Aimee," I say, using the Korean order of last name first. I shake her hand and we enter the café together.

The café is two floors and she leads me up to the second level. There are already three people sitting around a long table where someone has made a little paper sign that says "STWS MEETUP." There is a lady in a pink cardigan with headphones around her neck, not unlike the ones that Junho has; a man with more piercings in his ears than I can count; and a grandpa with hair as white as my jumpsuit.

Seri beelines straight for them. It suddenly occurs to me that maybe they've all met before. That maybe the people with STWS living in Seoul are all close and meet up all the time and I'll be the one random new person.

"Nice to meet you all," Seri says, bowing her head in greeting.

Or not. I follow suit, greeting everyone, feeling a little less out of place.

We all order drinks and wait a bit longer for anyone else to join us, introducing ourselves in the meantime. The lady in pink is named Han Mikyung, the man with the earrings is Lee Eunchul, and the grandpa is Jo Junghoon. I repeat the names in my head, committing them to memory, though I know I won't say them out loud. There's specific etiquette in Korean around calling older people by their names—how to do it, how not to do it, when to use titles instead—that I still feel somewhat awkward with, so I usually try to avoid it altogether if I'm not 100 percent sure.

"I'm Roh Aimee," I say when it's my turn. "I'm visiting from Canada."

"Canada! Were you born there?" Grandpa Junghoon asks. When I nod, he makes an impressed humming sound. "Your Korean is very good. Your parents must have taught you well."

In this context, I wonder if I should say something like, "Actually, my mom's not around and I'm wondering if she has STWS and is visiting me in my memories. Does anyone know if that's possible?" But I figure even at a meetup where we all have STWS, it's a weird way to begin.

So I just smile and nod. "Thank you. We speak a mix of Korean and English at home, but my dad's taught me well enough to speak Korean fluently."

There are still some words I don't get, though I'm usually able to fill them in by context. It takes extra concentration, though, especially in a group setting like this where everyone is speaking Korean, so I do my best to pay attention.

"Looks like no one else is joining us," Ms. Mikyung says. Her eyes keep drifting nervously around the ceiling. I glance up too but don't see anything out of the ordinary. "Has anyone been to these meetups before? It's my first time."

"It's mine too," Grandpa Junghoon says.

"I've been to a couple in Daegu where I live, but not in Seoul," Mr. Eunchul says. "I'm just here for a week for some work."

"I've been to every single one in Seoul," Seri says. "It's always a different group each time. They say STWS is rare, but there's still more of us than you'd think." She takes a sip of her iced chai latte and looks around the table. "My trigger is taste. I go back to certain memories when I eat or drink specific things."

Mr. Eunchul leans back in his seat, crossing his arms. "Must be easy to avoid, then. Just don't eat the things that'll take you back."

Seri nods. "It's definitely easier for me. But there are still some unexpected things. For example, I used to drink one matcha latte every day. It's never taken me back before, but one day suddenly, it did. So I changed my drink order." She holds up her chai latte, shaking it so the ice clatters around inside. "We're always making new memories, so that creates new triggers."

I never thought about that before. I look down at my own matcha latte. What other trigger smells will there be for me in the future that I can't even imagine right now?

"Mine is sight," Mr. Eunchul says. "Seeing certain things takes me back. Specifically colors."

"Colors?" Ms. Mikyung says.

"Yeah." He bites on the ice cube in his mouth, cracking it. "Say I go back to a memory in my old house. I don't have to see the house to go back to it. It's enough to see something that reminds me of it. The color of the rug in the living room, for example, or the color of the wallpaper."

"Colors. That's hard," Seri says.

Mr. Eunchul shrugs, swallowing his ice cube. "Yep."

"It's smell for me," Grandpa Junghoon says. "Scents take me back."

I feel an instant sense of kinship with this grandpa. "That's me too!" I say. He smiles warmly at me, eyes crinkling.

"They say people who react to scents have the most intense experience with time traveling," Seri says, "because our sense of smell is the one most connected to memories."

"Intense in what way?" I ask, curious.

"Different for everybody. Some say the memories are more vivid, or just longer in time."

Wow. Where are all these topics on the STWS forums? It's amazing just hearing about everyone's individual experiences. It's one thing to read about it, another to sit around a table and talk in real time, nodding along to the conversation. I think back to the Vancouver meetup. The best parts of that meeting were like this too. If only the whole thing could have felt as comfortable.

We all look at Ms. Mikyung.

"Only if you feel comfortable sharing," Seri says.

"Ah." Ms. Mikyung's eyes drift away from the ceiling, where she was staring again. "Mine is sound. Specifically, music."

I look up at the ceiling again and notice the speakers in the corner, playing K-pop. That explains why her eyes keep drifting up every few minutes. She's paying attention to the speakers every time the song changes.

Mr. Eunchul whistles. "That's hard. I can't live without music."

"Me neither," Ms. Mikyung whispers, so quiet I think only I heard her.

Seri pulls out a tablet from her backpack and lays it on the table. "Would people mind if I took notes during our chat? Nothing personal about anyone, just general conversation or facts about STWS that come up. I can share them at the end of the meetup and erase anything anyone isn't comfortable with."

We all exchange glances and nod, giving permission for her to take notes. It's a totally different feeling than when Cole was taking notes at the Vancouver meetup. Unlike Cole and his documentary, Seri not only has STWS, but she knows how to talk about it in a way that feels both smart and safe.

"Are you writing an essay or something?" Mr. Eunchul asks.

"I'm in computer engineering at Korea University and I want to build an app for people with STWS," Seri explains. "I mean, I can't believe it doesn't already exist. In this day and age? The forums are so outdated and not intuitive enough, and there's probably only a small percentage of people with STWS who actually visit them. But what if there was one app that combined the forums with other STWS resources and tips from professionals and a way for people to connect more naturally with each other? Like the connectivity of Tinder meets the self-help aspect of a meditation app. But for STWS."

Whoa. I've been here for less than thirty minutes and I feel like my mind is already being blown. "That is so genius," I say. "I would totally use that. And you're right . . . Why *doesn't* it exist yet?"

"Because nobody cares about STWS," Mr. Eunchul says matter-of-factly. "It doesn't affect enough people for the greater majority to give a shit or offer any substantial funding."

"People cared more in the olden days, but not necessarily in a good way," Grandpa Junghoon muses. "Those with STWS were historically seen as spectacles, followed around by crowds who wanted to see a show, or even taken into labs for invasive experiments. Of course, that's been made illegal for decades now. In many ways, we're lucky to have faded into the background as much as we have. There's not much for the general public to be interested in once they realize the only place we're time traveling to is our own memories and there's nothing they can gain from it themselves."

Silence falls around the table as we all take that in. As much as progress has been slow for STWS, it is true that we're lucky to live in a lifetime where we're not being actively chased down by people for our condition. I think back to when I was first diagnosed, how Appa refused to bring me into the hospital for any further studies. I wonder if part of the reason he was so adamant, and still is, is because of the history of how people with STWS were mistreated and abused. What Gomo said about stigma comes back to me too.

"Harabeoji, we've faded into the background so much we may as well be ghosts now," Mr. Eunchul says, shaking his head. "Nobody understands how disruptive our condition is and there are hardly any professionals out there who are trained to help."

"To accept help, you must first trust the person offering it," Grandpa Junghoon says. "How are you supposed to trust those professionals when there has been such a history of pain? You don't realize how good we have it now compared to back then."

"That's what the app will be for," Seri says. "Help for people with STWS from people with STWS. Who understands our condition more than us?"

"Actually," I say, half raising a hand as if asking permission to speak. "I feel like I don't understand my condition at all. And I was wondering . . ." I take a breath, trying to formulate the question that's been stirring in my mind for days. Now that I have to say it out loud, it suddenly feels totally absurd. They're definitely going to laugh at me. Or maybe they won't. I won't know until I ask. "Have any of you ever seen another traveler in your memory? Like someone who's not supposed to be there?"

"Of course," Ms. Mikyung answers immediately.

My eyes widen. I don't know what answer I was expecting, but it wasn't that. "Really? I couldn't find very much about it on the forums."

Seri types on her tablet, eyes going back and forth between me and Ms. Mikyung.

"I don't know about others, but I don't post very much on the forums myself. I don't like to share online," Ms. Mikyung says. "But in my experience, when two people with STWS happen to go back to a memory at the same time and place, of course they'll end up meeting there. It's inevitable."

"So if you see someone in a memory who doesn't belong, it means they're also someone with STWS traveling there," I say slowly.

"It happens more the older you get," Ms. Mikyung says. "You've lived more life so you have more overlapping memories with other STWS folks. It may not be common, but it happens."

Grandpa Junghoon smiles, sipping his black coffee. "I used to carry a deck of hwatu cards in my pocket so I could play go-stop with other travelers if we met in our memories. Sometimes it was a nicer way to pass the time than to see the past unfold again."

"Why'd you stop carrying them, Harabeoji?" Mr. Eunchul asks.

"Oh, one of us was always disappearing before we could finish a game. It got annoying."

My mind is spinning so fast, I feel like I should be the one taking notes. I take a peek at Seri's screen, where she's typing away about meeting other travelers in the memoryscape.

The memoryscape. I've never heard anyone use that term before. I didn't even know there were terms to know other than Sensory Time Warp Syndrome. Being here is making me realize how much I don't know about STWS, both presently and in terms of its history. All this time, I thought it was enough to scroll through the forums, fishing for answers, but I never knew how much there was to know, how deep my curiosity could go. Maybe I should have given the Vancouver meetups a second chance, when Cole wasn't there. I could have been having conversations like this the whole time.

"There's a lot that's unknown still about STWS," Seri says, noticing me staring at her tablet. She rotates the screen to show me, scrolling through her notes. "See? My research has shown that some people grow out of it after childhood, but others don't even develop it till they become adults. It seems random, doesn't it? And what about the memories we go back to? Sometimes they seem like core memories only, but I met someone the other day who only traveled back to the most mundane moments of his life. He'd be stuck watching his past self slice apples or wash the dishes until he was done. Why? I want to know everything."

I nod along at her passion, but Ms. Mikyung sighs, shaking her head.

"Aigoo, you're ambitious," she says. "Me? I just want to survive each day. I don't care about knowing everything about everything. I just want to understand myself enough to live my life and be happy."

I can't help but nod along at that too. As much as I feel swept up in Seri's desire for knowledge, I probably relate more to Ms. Mikyung, at least right now.

"But there's so much out there," Seri says. "Don't you want to know why people go where they go? Or see if the theory of time loops is true?"

I flinch at the mention of time loops. It's one thing to hear Cole talk about it as fodder for his documentary or even to hear Junho's friends discuss it in casual conversation. But to hear it from Seri, someone who takes STWS seriously and knows her stuff, makes me pause. What *does* everyone here think about it?

"That rumor where people get stuck in their memories and loop infinitely without returning to the present?" Mr. Eunchul says. "I don't know. That can't be real, can it?"

"Why not?" Seri says. "I've met some people who think it is. There are stories about it. And there are certainly enough unsolved missing person reports to warrant it."

"I actually heard a rumor of one recently," I say hesitantly. "They call him the Hapjeong Station Ghost. Some say he's a ghost, like the name says, but others think he's a person with STWS vanishing in and out of a memory. But I don't understand it. How would someone get stuck like that?"

"I don't know," Seri admits. "I've only heard speculations. I've never met anyone who's gone through it."

"I don't care about that. The only thing I want to know is how to stop vanishing," Ms. Mikyung says firmly. "The only thing I want to know is how to live my damn life normally."

At this, we all fall silent. The song on the speakers changes and Ms. Mikyung flinches.

"I want that too," I say, looking down at my hands. There are so many things I've never said out loud before, but to this group, it feels strangely natural. "I want to experience things without worrying that I'm going to ruin them by disappearing before they even happen. I want to feel like I'm not missing out on my own life. Honestly, I wish there was some kind of instant cure to take this all away."

I look up. Everyone is staring at me, and I can see it in

their eyes that they all understand exactly what I mean.

"There's no cure like that," Seri says quietly. "It is what it is."

Everyone looks down at their cups, now empty, and I know that in this too, we also understand exactly what she means.

KAKAO MESSENGER

Junho:

Hey! What are you up to today?
Want to get bingsu?

Aimee:

Hi, sorry for the late reply. I actually have a lot
on my mind today . . . Next time?

Junho:

Ofc no worries. Everything okay?

Aimee:

Yes yes, all good.

Aimee:

Sorry to miss out on bingsu. I love shaved ice
in all forms.

Junho:

Another day then? My treat for (unofficially)
losing the Great Elliptical Race.

Aimee:

Haha. Sounds good. I'll message you later ok?

Eighteen

I head back home on the subway, my brain swimming with information from today's meetup. There was just so much, I don't even know how to begin processing it all. Ms. Mikyung confirmed for me that it is possible to meet other travelers in your memories. Grandpa Junghoon even played go-stop with people he encountered in the past. So what does this mean about the woman I saw? What does it mean if that was really my mom?

Even with all the questions, there's an energy to them that I don't think I've ever felt before. Everyone at the meetup exchanged emails before we parted ways, and Seri said she would let us know if she has any updates on her app. I've always felt like STWS has isolated me from others, but today was the first day it made me feel like I was part of something bigger, something that connected me to people in a way that I've never thought I needed in the past.

I'm so lost in my thoughts that I don't realize I missed my transfer stop until we're already way past it. Shoot. I pull up my subway app and look at the map. I could get off and go back, but at this point it might take me longer to retrace my route. I could also transfer at Hongik University or Hapjeong Station instead.

Hapjeong Station.

A strange feeling runs down my spine. I stare at the station name on my phone screen. It's probably just because I was talking about the Hapjeong Station Ghost at the meetup that it's standing out to me right now.

It's just a ghost story, I remind myself. Bora loves ghost stories.

But then something else creeps into my head, something Eunchul said at the meetup. *Harabeoji, we've faded into the background so much we may as well be ghosts now.*

There's a word in Korean that strikes me now, repeating over and over in my head. *Seolma.* It's one of those Korean words that don't translate neatly into English, but it's something like "no way" or "could it be?"

I suddenly feel chilled to the bone and I wish I'd brought a jacket. I'm clearly reading too much into this. Jumping to conclusions. Making connections that aren't there.

But I can't shake the unsettled feeling in the pit of my stomach.

The subway stops at Hongik University. I stand up to transfer, hesitate, sit back down. The doors slide shut. We move on.

"The next stop is Hapjeong Station," the voice over the speakers announces.

I get off.

On the Hapjeong Station line two platform going toward Dangsan, there's a ghost that looks like a man with long black hair, just wandering around. He appears out of nowhere, crying, and then goes invisible again just like that.

Imagine everyone thinking you're a ghost when really, you're just a human trapped in some kind of weird memory loop.

Bora's and Yul's words replay in my mind as I walk along the platform, looking, feeling somewhat foolish. Seolma.

I'm probably wrong. I'm almost definitely wrong. It could be so many things. A trick of the light. An actual ghost. Who's to say they don't exist? But I still can't shake this feeling and I have to know.

So I wait. And wait. And wait, fully aware that I look like a loiterer or someone who's been badly stood up but refuses to go home.

Hapjeong Station is huge. What if I'm not even in the right spot? But no, Bora specifically said this platform, so I stay on this platform. I pull out my phone and take photos so it doesn't look like I'm doing nothing, making a mental note to get a replacement battery for my film camera soon.

The subway. Snap.

People moving up the stairs, sneakers scuffing the ground. Snap.

Another subway, pulling away, emptying the platform so it's just me and my phone. Snap.

And then, a flicker of movement.

Seolma.

I spot him through my phone camera first. Almost like a magic trick, a man who was not there a second ago appears in the screen. My breath catches in my throat, and I slowly lower my phone. He's standing by the subway platform screen doors, one hand pressed against his head. His hair is black and hanging to his shoulders. He's wearing a brown zip-up hoodie and jeans. He looks around Appa's age.

But the most noticeable thing about him is how he's not really . . . here. He's kind of flickering like a TV channel losing its signal.

For a moment, I'm rooted to the spot. I don't know what to say or do. Is he a ghost? Or is he what I think he is?

I snap out of it and run up to him, calling out, "Jeogiyo! Ajusshi!"

He hardly registers me. The flickering is getting more intense, like he's about to fade out to nothing at any moment. I need a way to grab his attention.

There's no time to be polite. I stand directly in front of him and look him straight in the eye. His are glassy, far away, but I hold them anyway, refuse to break eye contact. "Ajusshi, are you a ghost or are you someone with STWS?"

At the word *STWS*, his eyes lock on mine. They grow just a little bit clearer. I have his attention. The flickering subsides as he starts to look more solid again. "Who are you?" he asks, his voice gravelly.

"I'm Aimee and I have Sensory Time Warp Syndrome," I say. I speak in a rush, afraid to lose time, not sure how much we have. "I'm wondering if you do too, or if you're a ghost like they say."

"How long have I been gone for?" He shakes his head, like he's trying to remember.

"Do you have a phone?" I ask.

He fumbles in the pockets of his hoodie, pulls out a phone. Even as he turns it toward me, his hand flickers in and out.

I stare at the screen.

The phone says Jan 11, 2017, 9:07 p.m.

But . . . 2017 was years ago. Your phone is supposed to be stuck at the time when you leave for your memory, so that would have to mean he went in 2017 and didn't come back until now.

That can't be. Who goes to a memory that's years long? Maybe he just never restarted his phone since he came back so it's permanently stuck on that time. But no. If he was back here, his phone would have started working again, regardless of whether he restarted it or not, and the battery would be drained by now for sure.

A creeping dread runs down my spine.

Does this mean he's been stuck in a memory for years?

"Ajusshi, we should get you out of here," I say urgently.

"No, no, I need to see Yuri again. I promised I'd meet her here. She'll be waiting for me."

"Ajusshi, I think you've been stuck in a memory. If you

just restart your phone now, you'll see. We're not in 2017 anymore. We're—"

There's a musical jingle over the speakers, announcing the arrival of the subway.

The man lifts his face as it begins to pull into the station. He presses his palm against the platform screen doors, fingers fanning, and murmurs, "It felt like this."

And then he vanishes.

GOOGLE SEARCH HISTORY

STWS stuck in a memory

STWS time loop

STWS are time loops real

STWS how do you get stuck in a time loop

STWS how do you get out of a time loop

STWS how to find someone lost in a time loop

Nineteen

The cherry blossoms will be blooming soon in Seoul, but first the plum blossoms arrive.

Gomo and I go out on Sunday morning to see them. She tells me about a path along Cheonggyecheon, the stream that runs through downtown Seoul. "It's called Hadong Maesil Geori," she says. Hadong Plum Street.

She's excited. I can tell by the way she keeps counting down the subway stops on our way there. She says this is her favorite time of the year.

I wish I could be excited with her, but all I can think about is the Hapjeong Station Ghost. I haven't been able to get him out of my head. The theory of time loops burns in my mind. *That rumor where people get stuck in their memories and loop infinitely without returning to the present?* It's real. The rumors are real. I'm almost positive that's what was happening to the Hapjeong Station Ghost. He seemed to be trying to return to the present, only he kept glitching away like the past was trying to pull him back.

Short of a few dead chats on the forums, random articles

outlining all the conspiracy theories surrounding Benji Grey-Diaz's disappearance, and of course Cole's sensationalized documentary, I couldn't find much information in all my Google searching last night. Maybe I'm just not looking in the right places.

I ended up emailing Seri asking if she knows anything more about time loops and reading the *Hapjeong Station Ghost* webtoon that Bora mentioned, reaching for clues. But the webtoon is 100 percent fictional, a story about a ghost organization that assigns a different ghost to each subway station in Seoul to look for treasure buried in the tunnels, treasure that they all died looking for and can't peacefully pass into the afterlife until they find. It was a good story. But not what I was looking for.

I know the Hapjeong Station Ghost—the real one—isn't looking for buried treasure. He's looking for Yuri, whoever that is, and he's going back to his memories to find her. The look in his eyes haunts me, that glassy, faraway look like he's seeing something that's not there. It reminds me of that memory of my mom in Salt Spring Island, staring at the sailboat paintings for hours and hours.

I can't stop the whisper in my head, the one that started small but keeps sinking its claws deeper and deeper, not letting go.

What if my mom has STWS and when she left us, she didn't actually leave? What if she got stuck in a time loop instead? And what if all my recent disappearances have been a sign not just for me to find closure, but for me to go on this journey to find her?

"Aimee?" Gomo's voice breaks me out of my thoughts. "This is our stop."

We get off the subway.

It's a little overcast today, and I button up my beige corduroy jacket to stay warm. The stream is not too far from the station and soon we find ourselves on a path lined with white-blossomed trees. They smell fragrant and flowery, just the way you imagine spring would smell. I breathe it in, pause for a moment, my body on alert to see what will happen, and then exhale. We're okay here.

"Ah, yeppeuda," Gomo says, admiring the trees. "Aren't they pretty, Aimee? Remind me, do you have these in Vancouver too?"

"I think so," I say. "But everyone is mostly waiting for the cherry blossoms."

She nods. "That's like here too. But I like plum blossoms best."

Before she can continue, a voice says, "Misu, is that you?" A woman with curly hair walking from the opposite direction with a stroller stops when she sees Gomo. "Fancy running into you here!"

"Look who it is!" Gomo says, laughing. She turns to me, putting an arm around my shoulders. "Aimee, say hello. This is a teacher I work with at the elementary school."

I bow in greeting. "Annyeonghaseyo."

"This is my niece. She's visiting from Canada," Gomo says proudly.

"Ahh, she's pretty," the teacher says. "I'm here with my kids and grandchild."

The baby in the stroller makes a gurgling sound and Gomo leans down to look at him. "Oh my, what a handsome baby. You must be so in love!"

"So very." The teacher smiles. "Misu, you need to meet a man soon and get married so you can have kids and grandkids! A niece is great, but you need your own too, right?"

Gomo's smile grows a bit stiff. She straightens up and laughs, smoothing it over quickly. "Don't worry about me, I have everything I need!"

"Still, don't lose hope. It's not too late, even at your age." The teacher nods adamantly. I frown, not liking the way she's looking at Gomo, eyes tinged with pity. They chat for a few more seconds about the blossoms and then we wave goodbye as she rolls off with the stroller to join her kids.

I stare after her, waiting until she's out of earshot, and then I look at Gomo, who has gone back to slowly strolling along the path. I hurry to catch up with her.

"Did what that teacher said bother you, Gomo?" I ask.

"Don't worry about me, Aimee, I hear it all the time," she says. "It's common for a single woman of my age to get comments like that. But I just let it roll right off my back now."

"Do you even want the things she was talking about?"

I ask. "Marriage and kids and grandkids?"

She thinks for a moment. "Well. I'm not sure. Who knows what the future will hold, but truthfully, I've never once in my life felt the desire for a romantic partner. Some might say it's odd, but I don't think it is. It's just me. I've never felt like I was lacking in life when it already feels so full. And as much as I love kids, I'd say between my students and you, I get my fair share of spending time with some great ones."

She smiles, holds her hand out. I take it, squeezing.

"Well, your students are lucky to have you," I say, sincere.

"And you?"

"I'm the luckiest." I squeeze her hand again. "Now tell me why you like plum blossoms the best."

"Ah!" She lets go of my hand to hold her arms out wide, as if embracing the trees before her. "Plum blossoms start blooming when the weather is still cold. Some say they symbolize hope and perseverance because they live between two seasons: enduring through the winter and welcoming the spring. They are a sign that warmer days are coming. Of course, then the cherry blossoms arrive and steal all the attention." She laughs. "But I like cherry blossoms too. Hopefully you might get to see those while you're here too."

"I like that," I say. "I've never thought about plum blossoms before."

I wish more than ever that I had my film camera with me to capture this scene. But maybe it's okay that I don't.

Maybe it's okay to just enjoy the moment without trying to preserve it for later.

The wind blows and the blossoms rustle. I close my eyes and breathe in deep. The scent is sweet. If I have to live with STWS, please at least bring me back to moments like this.

I can't help thinking about it again. STWS, my mom, time loops. We walk along the stream and I stare at the blossoms, remembering the flower shop information that Nikita found for me. If anyone would know what really happened to my mom, maybe it would be my grandparents.

"Gomo," I say. "Have you ever been to Gwangju before?"

"Gwangju? Why so suddenly? I've never been."

"I heard that's where my grandparents are from. On my mom's side."

"Oh?" Gomo pauses. "Now that you mention it, I do think I remember that. Your mom was born in Gwangju and moved to Seoul as a child."

"How far is it?"

"It's probably about three or four hours south of Seoul by car. Or even faster on the KTX high-speed train." She raises her eyebrows. "Why?"

There's a part of me that wants to tell Gomo everything. But somehow, saying that I think my mom might be stuck in a time loop and I want to go meet my grandparents to find out the truth feels too overwhelming. I'm still processing the idea myself. I can't talk about it yet, not even with her, so instead, I go with a half-truth.

"I'm just curious about where my mom came from. I think I'd like to visit if I can."

"Hmm. I don't know." Her brow furrows, concerned. "It's one thing for you to explore Seoul on your own, but to travel to another city? I don't think your dad would be comfortable with that, and I wouldn't be able to take you myself with work. I can call him tonight and see what he thinks, though."

My stomach sinks. Appa will never say yes if he knows I want to go to Gwangju to do anything related to my mom. "Could you maybe ask him without mentioning my grandparents or my mom at all? Maybe you don't even have to say Gwangju. Maybe you can just say I want to take a day trip to another city nearby."

My voice gets faster, more anxious, as I speak. She frowns, looking at me like she's trying to read my face. I press my lips together, not giving anything away.

"I can't promise to withhold information from him, Aimee," she says finally. "He's your dad. When's the last time you spoke to him anyway?"

"Um . . . a few days ago. That day we had sujebi."

"Does he know you've been having some hard days here in Korea?"

I blink and remember how Gomo found me in my room that day, curled up in bed all afternoon with the blinds drawn. "What do you mean? I'm fine," I say. The words scrape against my throat.

Gomo sighs. "I'll talk to him. I'll call him when we get home, okay?"

I still feel uncertain about how Appa will respond, but if Gomo's giving her best, that's the most I can ask for. I nod. "Okay."

"Now let's enjoy these blossoms."

We walk to an area where the plum blossoms are dark pink. The wind blows again and blossoms scatter into the sky. I know I told myself that I would just enjoy the moment, but I can't help but take a photo in my mind.

Snapshot: if ever there was such a thing as angels on earth, they would look like plum blossom trees, branches spread like wings, pink and white petals falling like feathers to the ground. Gomo reaches up to catch one. I do too. They slip through our fingers and we hold each other instead. Hands holding, arms swinging, blossoms blooming. We carry on.

I realize the next day that I only have one week left in Seoul. I can't believe how fast the time is going. Even though my head is still swimming with thoughts, I put a pause on everything for a moment to take a break and buy souvenirs.

I consider asking Junho to go with me. It's been a few days since I last saw him outside Gomo's apartment, and I haven't been very responsive to his texts lately. I said I'd get back to him about getting bingsu and I never did. Not because I don't want to see or talk to him, but because I've been distracted by everything on my mind. In the end, I decide that I just need some time on my own today, but I promise myself that I'll message him soon.

My shopping begins at Insadong, a neighborhood known for its art and culture and traditional souvenir shops. It feels nice to wander by myself, walking around the spiraling walkway of Ssamzigil, the multilevel market complex, and peeking into all the shops there. There are so many good ones. I find a hand-painted paper fan for Nikita, a small watercolor set attached to a key chain for Russell, and a magnet in the shape of a soccer ball that says "Goal!" on it in Korean for Mr. Riaga.

For Appa, I find a dark green mug at a ceramics shop to replace the one he has at home with the spider crack. I hesitate for a minute before buying it, not sure if he'll want to switch mugs. He's had that old one forever. But I get it anyway and decide he can decide for himself whether he wants to use it or not. I also find a small banchan plate painted with plum flowers and buy it for Gomo.

Seoul is alive. I let myself be carried along its bustling streets, feeling the pulse of the city. People wearing rented hanboks pass me, colorful skirts billowing as they stop to take photos, finger hearts in the air. I stop to buy a couple of chicken skewers from a food stall, lathered in savory sauce, and then some gyeran bbang, thick, fluffy sweet bread filled and topped with a whole egg. All the people working at the food stalls are precise and efficient, whipping out the delicious street food perfectly each time like they've been doing this their whole lives. Maybe some of them have.

I'm going to miss this place. The thought comes and settles in my gut, bittersweet. I wish spring break was longer. I wish I had more time to just soak it all in.

After I finish souvenir shopping, I find a photo store and pop in to get a replacement battery for myself and a couple of extra film rolls. At the cash register, I notice a display of blue pocket-sized notebooks with the words "My Brilliant Ideas" written across the cover. I pick one up, thumb through it, and slide it onto the counter. "I'll take this too," I tell the shop employee.

On my way home, I take a detour at Hapjeong Station. I stand at the platform where I met the ajusshi last time and wait to see if he might appear.

He doesn't, and eventually I leave, disappointed.

I make sure to hide all the gifts inside my tote bag before going home. Gomo should be back from work by the time I get there and I want to save the banchan plate for the day before I leave. I punch in the code on the front door and push it open, calling, "Gomo! I'm home!"

"Oh, Aimee, are you here?" Her voice comes from the living room.

I take off my shoes, noticing a pair of men's shoes next

to Gomo's. I haven't seen them here before, but they look somehow familiar. Maybe Mr. Kim is here? "Do you have a visitor?" I ask, walking into the living room.

I freeze. It's not Mr. Kim sitting next to Gomo on the couch, holding a cup of barley tea.

It's Appa.

"Hi, Aimee," he says. "Surprise."

Twenty

"Appa? What are you doing here?" I'm so shocked, I don't know what else to say.

He looks uncertain, almost embarrassed, like he has no idea what he's doing here himself. There's a suitcase next to him with a luggage tag in the shape of a cantaloupe hanging off the handle, a matching set with my honeydew one.

Gomo stands up from the couch, ushering me to sit down next to Appa. I sit and she brings me a cup of tea.

"Here, drink this bori cha," she says. "You're so surprised your face has lost all its color!"

Appa clears his throat, probably thinking he should explain himself right about now. "I spoke to your aunt on the phone last night and she convinced me to come visit for a week."

I stare at Gomo. I know she said she was going to talk to Appa yesterday, but I didn't know she was going to actually bring him here in person.

"I told him that you want to see other cities in Korea," Gomo says. "I can't go with you myself, but your dad can, and this could be a fun opportunity for the two of you to spend some time together."

She looks hopeful.

I turn to Appa. "What about the auto shop? I thought you couldn't take that much time off."

"We were able to work it out for one week, so I booked the next flight out," he says.

That's right. If Gomo called him yesterday and he's already arrived today, he must have moved fast to get a flight. Silence settles between us as we all grasp for what to say next. What is there to say? Appa is here, in the flesh, like he climbed out of our FaceTime call and stepped into the living room, just as weathered as he looked on my phone screen.

"Hyunwoo, you must be tired from the flight," Gomo says. "Why don't you take a quick nap before dinner in my room?"

"Oh. Okay. Sounds good, Nuna," he says. He gives me a small smile and then follows her into the room, taking his suitcase with him.

Nuna. It's so strange to hear Appa call someone older sister. So strange that he's someone's younger brother. That he's anyone else other than Appa, my dad, in Vancouver with his cracked coffee cup and grease-stained hands. I knew all this in my head, of course, but to see him here so suddenly after being here without him is jarring. I don't know what to do with any of it.

Gomo comes out of her bedroom, clicking the door shut.

She sits down next to me, looking apologetic.

"I'm sorry if that was very shocking for you. It seems like it was."

"I just can't believe he's here," I say. "What did you say to him on the phone?"

She pauses. "I didn't tell him why you wanted to go to Gwangju specifically since you seem hesitant for him to know. I just told him that his daughter wants to see more of Korea, Gwangju included, and it would be something to consider to take her on this trip himself before she goes off to university. These kinds of opportunities are only going to get rarer."

I sigh. "Gomo . . ."

"This might not be what you were imagining, and I know there's been some distance between you two these days. But he's here, right?"

I look down at the cup of bori cha in my hands, warming my palms. I'm not mad at Gomo for inviting him. I just don't know how to feel about it. Searching for my mom and learning more about STWS seemed so much easier when he wasn't around. He hasn't even done anything yet, but just his presence being here makes it feel like a hurdle I have to jump to keep doing what I want to do. What I need to do.

But Gomo's right. He's here, regardless of how I feel about it.

And no matter what, I'm going to find a way to finish what I started.

* * *

That night, Mr. Kim and Junho come over for dinner.

"Hyunwoo!" Mr. Kim embraces Appa in a giant hug, slapping his back at least ten times. "It's been so long. I didn't think you were coming into town!"

"Last-minute plans," Appa says. He looks a bit squished and awkward in the hug, but there's a genuine grin on his face. "It's good to see you too, Hyung."

"You remember my son," Mr. Kim says, patting Junho on the back.

Junho bows in greeting and then looks over at me and smiles. It's hesitant at first, like he's checking to see if I'm okay, like he felt the distance I've been unintentionally putting between us. I never did get a chance to message him like I told myself I would. But then I smile back and all his hesitation disappears, going warm. My stomach flutters.

"Hi," he says.

"Hi," I say back.

Appa glances between the two of us, raising his eyebrows. It's weird to see them in the same room, like worlds colliding, even though technically, they already knew each other. I clear my throat and look away, busying myself with setting the table.

Gomo has prepared a Korean barbecue spread for us. The table is crowded with bowls of rice and piles of lettuce, kimchi and perilla leaves, the mouthwatering smell of grilled meat wafting up from plates of samgyupsal and galbi. Junho and I sit next to each other with our dads across the table and Gomo at the head. I inhale all the scents in the kitchen, bracing myself for a moment, and then relax.

We dig in.

I grab a piece of lettuce and lay on top of it a piece of samgyupsal, a spoonful of rice, and a dollop of ssamjang, a thick spicy paste made with a mix of doenjang and gochujang that goes perfectly with Korean barbecue, folding it all up into a little pouch and stuffing it in my mouth. The flavor combination is explosive. Gomo's food is hands down the best.

"Nuna, I forgot how much I love your homemade ssamjang," Appa says, actually looking a little emotional as he chews.

"Tastes just like how our mom used to make it, right?" Gomo says proudly. "Took me a while to figure that one out. I could never quite get the ratio of soybean paste to chili paste right until recently."

"So what brings you to Seoul, Hyunwoo?" Mr. Kim asks, putting a giant scoop of rice into his lettuce and layering it with perilla leaves. "I thought you weren't coming when Aimee arrived alone."

"We're going to go on a trip," Appa says. He says it matter-of-factly like it was his idea all along, as if he wasn't completely against me coming to Korea in the first place. The comment irks me, but I stuff a lettuce wrap in my mouth and say nothing.

"A trip?" Junho looks at me, his eyes lighting up. "That sounds fun. Where are you going?"

"Um . . ." I chew slowly, swallowing my food. "Well, Gwangju was one of the places."

I have no idea what other cities are in this supposed trip of ours. How exactly did Gomo phrase it to Appa?

"And Busan," Gomo jumps in. "Also a stop in Boseong while you're in Gwangju. The green tea fields are beautiful."

"Yes, all of those places," Appa says. If Gwangju rings any bells for him, he doesn't show it. In fact, he looks more relaxed and comfortable than I've seen him in a long time. That ssamjang really must be magic.

"I've never been to any of those places," Junho says, casting a look at his dad. "How come we don't do any father-son trips like that?"

"Ya inma, what do you think this whole Seoul trip is?" he says, reaching across the table to knuckle Junho in the head. "Besides, we might head down to Busan too for a couple days before we leave to visit your cousins. They just moved there."

"Really?" Junho sits up straighter, looking between me and his dad. "Aimee, maybe we'll be there at the same time!"

"They've been hanging out," Mr. Kim says to Appa.

I sip my water, trying to be casual, glancing at Appa over the rim to see his reaction. He just smiles and nods.

"If you're going to Busan too, maybe you should just join us on our trip," he says. "Make it a group thing."

"We wouldn't want to intrude on your time together," Mr. Kim says, waving a hand in the air.

"I don't mind. Aimee?" Appa says, looking at me.

The thought of searching for my mom while on a trip with just Appa has been majorly stressing me out since he arrived. How am I going to do anything without him knowing? And if he did know, he would definitely try to stop me. He doesn't even like talking about my mom. But if Mr. Kim and Junho are there too, it might be easier to evade his attention. And there would be a lot less awkward silence.

And, well, Junho would be there.

Underneath the table, my hand brushes against Junho's. He brushes my hand back and then, so swift that my breath catches in my throat, he hooks his pinkie finger around mine. Nobody else notices. I squeeze his pinkie back.

"I don't mind," I say.

"Well then, should I rent a car for all of us?" Mr. Kim says enthusiastically. "Junho just helped me set up an account on that Spot It app."

"Spotify, Appa," Junho says.

"Right, right, Spotify. I can make us a playlist now! Put all the classics on there."

Gomo clicks her tongue, shaking her head. "Your idea of the classics are all Celine Dion songs, Sungmin. Leave the playlists to the young kids."

Mr. Kim looks hurt. "Celine Dion *is* classic. Anyway,

I'll drive. It'll be just like old times, right, Hyunwoo?"

Appa smiles. "Yeah. That sounds good."

"Too bad Misu can't join us too."

Gomo shakes her head. "Don't feel bad for me, feel bad for these poor kids who will have to listen to hours of Celine Dion albums in the car."

Appa laughs. I blink at him. Seriously, who is this man and what did he do with my dad? When was the last time I ever saw him laugh like that, so light and carefree?

Gomo leans over and whispers to me, "I'm sorry I got you into this." She pats my shoulder. "Good luck."

I exchange a glance with Junho, our pinkies still looped together beneath the table. He hides his smile behind his water glass, taking a sip. "Thanks, Gomo," I say, but I'm thinking maybe this trip won't be so bad after all.

ROAD TRIP ITINERARY

DAY 1:
- Junho and Mr. Kim to pick us up in the morning
- Head to Boseong
- Gwangju for the night

DAY 2:
- Day in Gwangju (ideas for how to sneak away from Appa to see grand-parents: say I'm not feeling well so he leaves me at the Airbnb, pretend to get lost in a crowded place and run away, ~~tell him the truth~~, go out to buy snacks but secretly go to the flower shop instead)
- Head to Busan at night

DAY 3:
- Full day in Busan
- Junho and Mr. Kim to visit family
- Me and Appa to have father-daughter bonding time (. . .)

DAY 4:
- Last day in Busan
- Head back to Seoul

Twenty-One

The next morning, Mr. Kim and Junho come to pick us up bright and early in the rental car. We spent the better part of last night after dinner making last-minute travel plans, booking Airbnbs, and mapping out our route. Everyone still looks sleepy when we pile into the car, Appa in the front seat, me and Junho in the back.

Junho's hair is tousled like he literally just rolled out of bed, his headphones looped around his neck. "Morning," he says when he sees me, trying to flatten it with one hand with a self-conscious smile.

Sleepy Junho is a sight I never knew I needed until now. I want to tell him that his messy hair is fine, it suits him, and actually it even looks kind of cute. I'm so tempted to run my fingers through it, but I'm hyperaware of the fact that both our dads are sitting in the front.

"Morning," I say, buckling my seat belt. I can't help but glance over at him every few seconds, memorizing the details of his bedhead.

He nudges my foot with his. "Stop staring," he mouths to me.

I try to look ahead with a straight face, but when I glance back at him a second later, we both can't help but grin.

"All right, everyone, first stop, coffee. Second stop, Boseong, and then we'll spend the night in Gwangju," Mr. Kim says, adjusting his sunglasses. "Questions? Concerns?"

"Can I be DJ?" Junho asks.

"No, you already know I made a playlist. Aimee's dad and I will be taking turns as DJ."

"I should have never made him his own Spotify account," Junho grumbles.

Gwangju, *tonight*. My stomach churns at the thought that soon, we're going to be in the same city as my grandparents, one step closer to finding my mom. I breathe in deep, try to stay calm. Whatever happens, happens.

We make a quick stop at a 7-Eleven, where we grab coffee, water bottles, triangle kimbap, and snacks for the car. True to his word, Mr. Kim plays Celine Dion. Junho swears she's the reason why he immigrated to Canada.

"Junho's mom always used to complain about how loud I played my music when I drove," Mr. Kim says, frowning. "She loves nitpicking everything I do."

Junho tenses in his seat. "Appa, come on. She's not that bad."

"Not that bad? Aimee, tell me, is this music loud to you?"

"Um . . ." I'm not sure what to say. Junho looks absolutely mortified.

"She's always going on and on about how I'm going to

get in an accident one day," Mr. Kim says. Judging by the expression on Junho's face, I get the impression that this is a rant he's heard many times before. "But if anything was going to get me into an accident, it was her constant back-seat driving! Don't even get me started on how she—"

"Appa, tell us about how you and Aimee's dad used to go on road trips when you were younger," Junho says in a rush.

"Oh yeah, those were the days," Mr. Kim says, his frown perking into a smile. Junho's shoulders relax a bit, topic successfully diverted. "It was Misu and me going out with our friends, and Hyunwoo over here would beg and cry for us to take him along. So we had to babysit him on our trips."

"I didn't beg," Appa says, cheeks turning pink. There's something about seeing my dad embarrassed that embarrasses *me*, like it's not something I'm supposed to witness.

"He definitely begged," Mr. Kim says. "And he always wanted to play the loudest rap music in the car. He would bring along his prized possession—his Jay-Z CD—and play it in the car."

What.

"Appa, you liked Jay-Z?" I say incredulously.

"Worshipped is probably a better word," Mr. Kim laughs.

"He is a rap genius," Appa says. He grabs Mr. Kim's phone, starts scrolling through Spotify, a Jay-Z song coming on over the speakers. He leans his head back, closes his eyes. "Everyone, be quiet and listen."

Now I'm almost positive that this man in the car is not actually my dad. But come to think of it, whenever I would visit him at the auto shop, there would always be rap music playing in the background, and more often than not, Jay-Z. I always thought it was one of the other guys playing their songs. Not Appa.

Do I even know him at all?

An unsettled feeling begins to spread in my stomach the farther we drive, the closer we get to Gwangju. Maybe I haven't thought this through enough. The whole going to Gwangju and visiting my grandparents thing. The most I've planned is that I'll somehow slip away during our time in the city and visit It's a Good Flower Day. And then . . .

And then?

I've run through a dozen different scenarios in my head, a hundred different opening lines. But I have no idea how it'll actually go.

The drive to Boseong Green Tea Fields takes about four hours plus a lunch stop, which means that I have way too much time to sink deeper and deeper into my thoughts. It's a Good Flower Day. My mom. The Hapjeong Station Ghost and the woman in white in my memory. By the time we arrive at the fields, I've barely registered any of the conversations or the food we stopped to eat. The only thing in my brain is Jay-Z and my own worries spiraling away.

Mr. Kim parks and we get out of the car.

"Welcome to the tea fields!" Mr. Kim says. "I've never been here myself, but your aunt said we couldn't miss it."

We make our way to the front entrance, walking through a forest pathway to get there. Appa and Mr. Kim walk ahead and I trail behind, still lost in my thoughts. Junho keeps pace with me, glancing at the side of my face.

"Hey," he says, nudging me lightly in the arm. "Where are you?"

"Um . . . Boseong Green Tea Fields? Is this a trick question?"

"I mean, where are you here?" He lightly taps my forehead with one finger. "You got really quiet in the car and it looks like you've gone somewhere else." He looks worried. "Is it because of my dad? Sorry about him. I wish he wouldn't complain about my mom like that, especially in front of other people."

"No, no, it's not because of that," I say.

"Then what's up?"

"It's nothing. Don't worry about it."

I give him a reassuring smile, but this time he doesn't smile back. His brow furrows, like he's trying to figure out what he's missing, why I'm holding back.

I'm about to tell him again that everything is really fine when I hear Appa laugh up ahead at something Mr. Kim said. He's been laughing a lot here, so different than at home, where he's always drifting away. It suddenly hits me that I must look the way Appa does when he goes to that place in his mind where I can't follow. I've seen him do it hundreds of times, but I never realized I do the exact same thing.

I know how it feels to be on the other side of that. I don't want to do the same thing to someone I care about.

"Actually, it's not nothing," I say, taking a deep breath and lowering my voice. "To be honest, the whole reason we're on this road trip to begin with is because I told Gomo I want to go to Gwangju. It's the city where my mom is from and where my grandparents might still own a flower shop."

"Is it for your photography project?" Junho asks.

Ah. Right. The photography project that I made up where I take photos of places important to my family. I nearly forgot all about that. I hesitate and then nod, because it's easier to stick to that story than to explain the truth. "Yes."

"But why do you look so anxious about it?"

"I've never met my grandparents before. I want to visit, but I don't know what it'll be like to see them." *Or ask them questions about my mom and potential time loops*, I add silently to myself. "Also, I don't want my dad to know. He doesn't like talking about my mom and I feel like he won't approve."

"I see." Junho nods slowly. "Do you want me to go with you to the flower shop? We can ditch our dads and go together. We'll say we just want to go shopping or something. Dads hate shopping."

"Really?" I stop walking. "You'd do that?"

"I said I was here for you, right?"

My heart does a strange thing, doing synchronized somersaults with my stomach. "Right."

I start walking again, feeling a little lighter, knowing I won't have to face my grandparents alone. And the idea to tell our dads we're going shopping! That's way smarter than anything I've come up with so far. We approach the ticket booth and pay our entrance fee, and then we enter into the fields. My breath catches.

Green, everywhere, as far as the eye can see.

Rows of green tea shrubs stretch out horizontally before us, long and rolling, sloping upward like a mountain. Trails run alongside the shrubs, stretching up into a viewpoint promising to overlook the fields, cradled by forest. It looks like a postcard—no, better than a postcard. It looks like a painting. A dream. If peace were a place.

I can see why Gomo likes it here.

Junho and I follow the trail to walk between the shrubs, our dads going up ahead to the viewpoint. I reach into my tote bag and pull out my camera. I made sure to reload the battery last night as well as a fresh roll of film in preparation for moments just like this.

"How's the webtoon going, by the way?" I ask, snapping a photo of the fields.

"It's going," Junho says, fingers absent-mindedly trailing along the green tea leaves as we weave through the shrubs. "And by that, I mean it's not going at all." He sighs. "I don't know how anyone comes up with a good story idea. Where do they go to get them? And how do I get there?"

"Have you ever thought about collaborating with a writer? Like you do the art and someone else writes the story?"

"I'd be open to a collab. Zack's offered. He does some writing, but I'm not sure if our styles match up. You know, I had this amazing dream last night that I got sucked into a computer and there were all these monsters there, mutated from digital data. Some were allies, some were evil, and I had to fight off all the evil ones. And I thought, wow, this could be it. This could be The Story. But then I message my friends and Yul goes, 'Isn't that Digimon?'"

He slaps a hand against his forehead, shaking his head. "I'm just not very original. I don't know. Maybe I should consider letting Zack handle the story."

"I think you'll get it one day," I say.

"Thanks," he sighs. "That's nice of you."

"I'm not just saying it to be nice." I think back to the day we met at the kalguksu shop, before I knew Junho was Junho, when he was just the boy with the headphones. "Remember when we first met in Myeongdong? I actually saw you go into the restaurant. You were listening to music and you looked like you were daydreaming, like you were just letting your feet carry you while your mind was in another world."

Junho makes a face. "Yeah, my dad said one day I'm going to get mugged if I keep walking around without paying attention like that."

I laugh. "What I mean is, you're already an artist. You dream and you imagine and you make things. Remember what you said about art? How it makes you feel present and most like yourself? I know you'll find the story one day because art belongs with the artist, and it will make its way home to you eventually. I'm sure of it."

He stops walking and looks at me, serious. His gaze is piercing, and it makes me suddenly self-conscious. I clear my throat, tucking a strand of hair behind my ear. "What's wrong?"

He doesn't say anything for a moment and then he holds out his hand. "Can I have your hand for a second?"

My cheeks warm. I slowly lay my hand over his. Even though I'm not holding my breath, it feels like I am, like the entire green tea fields around us are, and all I can hear is my heartbeat drumming in my chest. He flips my hand over so my knuckles are resting against his palm and then he takes a pen from his pocket. He presses the ink to my wrist and draws. I let him, watching, a single Korean pear slowly blooming on my wrist, surrounded by flowers.

I blink, looking up at him. "This is . . ."

"I don't know if you remember, but I drew this on you when we first met," he says, hand still holding mine. "My dad was yelling at me for drawing all over myself again. He hated it when I did that, thought it was the most annoying thing. And then my mom came in to defend me, telling him to leave me alone, and they were just screaming at each other in public. All because of me. I was this close to crying when you noticed and told me you wanted one too. I never forgot it, and even now you keep encouraging me."

"I remember," I say. "I didn't want to wash it off."

His brown eyes go bright. "So you *do* remember."

The part about his parents fighting and Junho almost crying, I don't. When I visited the memory, it began with me sticking out my arm, wanting Junho to draw on it. The before part, I forgot. I guess that's how memories are, even for someone like me who can go back and visit pieces of them. Some you hold on to tight, some you lose to time. Some you find again in the present in a new and different way.

"I want to remember this too." I let go of his hand and hold up my camera.

"What should I do?" he says.

I raise it to my eye. "Just be here."

Snapshot: the boy with the ink-stained fingers, he is a letter tucked into an envelope of green tea leaves. A letter of art, a letter of love. He smiles.

I take the picture, but I know I won't need it to remember this moment.

MR. KIM'S SPOTIFY PLAYLIST

(AKA SONGS LISTENED TO ON REPEAT IN THE CAR)

RECENTLY PLAYED:

"It's All Coming Back to Me Now"—Celine Dion

"How Does a Moment Last Forever"—Celine Dion

"Because You Loved Me"—Celine Dion

"My Heart Will Go On"—Celine Dion

Twenty-Two

By the time we arrive in Gwangju—after hiking up to the viewpoint of the fields, after green tea ice cream and Junho buying one too many tea souvenirs for his mom and brother, after another hour in the car with Celine Dion's greatest hits—all the earlier peace I was feeling has melted away and the nerves come back, stronger than ever.

We're here. The same city as my grandparents.

The plan is to spend the night here, have a day in the city tomorrow, and then head to Busan after dinner, which will be about a three-hour drive. It doesn't give me a ton of time to visit the flower shop, especially since the rest of the day speeds by with dinner plans and Airbnb check-ins. By the time we're through with it all, It's a Good Flower Day is closed.

They open again tomorrow at 10:00 a.m. Junho and I make plans to head there early, telling our dads that we want to check out the shopping area in the morning and will meet them back here for lunch. As Junho predicted, they don't insist on joining us to shop.

We settle for the night in our two-bedroom Airbnb, me

in one room, Junho and Mr. Kim in the other, and Appa on the pull-out couch. Junho and Mr. Kim decide to go on a convenience store run to get some cup ramyeon and I stay behind with Appa as he sets up his bed.

"You can take the room if you want and I can sleep out here," I say.

"No, no. It's okay." He sits down on the pulled-out couch with a content sigh. "What did you think of the green tea fields?"

I sit down on the couch too, cross-legged. "I loved it. You?"

"It was nice. More exercise than I thought it would be, though. I can't even remember the last time I went on a hike."

I realize it's the first time since Appa arrived in Korea that it's just the two of us. Strangely, it doesn't feel as awkward as I thought it would. If anything, it feels comfortable, familiar in a nice way. I tuck my knees up, hugging them to my chest.

"Have you been to Gwangju before?" I ask. I venture cautiously, but he stays open, relaxed.

"Me? No. I never had a chance." He pauses for a moment. "Your mom was originally from here, actually. Before she moved to Seoul."

My heart thuds in my chest. Appa never brings up my mom first. "Really?"

"Yeah."

I wonder if he knows that my grandparents moved back

here. I want to ask, but then I would have to tell him how I know that, and I'm not sure how I would even begin to explain.

"Gomo says you had a disappearance in Seoul," Appa says.

That surprises me. Not that Gomo told him, but that Appa is bringing it up. "Yeah."

"Are you okay?"

"I'm . . . not sure."

He glances at me and smiles a complicated smile, at once somber and encouraging. "You will be. You're a strong, smart girl."

I look down at my feet and then back up at him. I take a leap. "What do you think my mom would have thought about it?"

"Thought about what?"

"Me disappearing. STWS."

He goes quiet, his smile fading. "I don't know," he says.

"I remember she used to be kind of spacey," I say. "Do you think—"

"It was a long time ago," Appa interrupts. His face shutters and he looks like the Appa I know again, Vancouver Appa, closed off and distant. "Who knows what she would have thought?"

Before I can think of a response, the front door swings open, and Mr. Kim yells, "Who wants cup noodles?"

That night I crawl into bed, staring at It's a Good Flower

Day on Naver Maps. It's a twenty-five-minute walk from where we're staying. I was in charge of finding the Airbnb and I made sure to choose the closest one I could. I text Nikita.

Me:

I'm in Gwangju. Going to the flower shop tomorrow.

Nikita:

Omg.

Nikita:

Good luck. You got this.

I turn off my phone, holding it against my chest.
I hope she's right.

Morning comes and I feel like I haven't slept at all.

I was tossing and turning all night, dreaming of subway station ghosts and closed flower shop doors and the woman in white at the ocean, turning her face toward me but always disappearing before I can see who she is.

I meet Junho at the front door, still feeling groggy, and we step out into the day.

It's gray outside and a little drizzly. We should have brought umbrellas, but we make do without, walking under the awnings of the storefronts we pass. I'm wearing my camera around my neck, but I tuck it inside my jacket to keep it dry.

"Thanks for coming with me," I say to Junho. "It's a bit of a walk."

"Don't worry, I wore good shoes," he says. "How'd you sleep last night?"

"Not great," I sigh.

"Nervous about meeting your grandparents?"

"Yeah. I don't know what I'm going to say." I pause, glancing over at the side of his face. It's only been a short time of knowing Junho, but everything I've told him in that time, he's been understanding about. Maybe there's no reason to hide things from him any longer. I take a deep breath and confess, "I'm actually hoping they might be able to tell me where my mom is."

"Oh wow." His eyes widen. "That's pretty huge."

"It is."

"I didn't realize you were looking for her." He grows thoughtful, connecting the pieces. "Your photography project about your family?"

"More like a project to find my mom." I smile weakly. "Sorry I wasn't more up-front about it sooner. There wasn't ever a photography project."

"Ah." He nods. "It's okay."

"Sorry," I say again, guilty.

He stops walking, resting his hand gently on my shoulder and turning me to face him. "Hey, don't feel bad. I get why it might be hard to bring that up to someone you just met.

Or re-met, I guess I should say. That's a really personal thing." He smiles. "Besides, if you didn't tell me about the photography project, I would have never offered to be your assistant and we wouldn't have hung out, would we?"

"I think I rejected your offer to be my assistant, though?"

"Yes, and I'm still recovering from that sting, obviously. But that was the beginning, wasn't it?"

I soften and smile back, the guilt ebbing away. "Yeah. It was."

Junho thinks for a moment. "Maybe you should bring your grandma and grandpa something," he suggests. "My mom always says I should never go empty-handed when I go see my grandparents. And it might help with the nerves, to have a gift to focus your attention on."

"That's a good idea. What do you usually bring?"

"Nothing major. Maybe some fruit or a drink."

We stop by a CU and I buy a couple of cartons of strawberry milk for my grandparents, plus two tuna-filled triangle kimbap for me and Junho since we didn't have breakfast. We eat in the convenience store, though I can only stomach half my kimbap. Coming clean to Junho was a weight off my shoulders, but I still feel a churning anxiety about seeing my grandparents. We finish up and keep walking. The rain is starting to come down harder.

And then I see it. A sunny yellow sandwich board that says "It's a Good Flower Day! Come on in." My eyes trail from the sign to the store it's in front of.

There it is. The flower shop. From out here, I can see people through the window, moving around inside. It's unmistakably the grandma and grandpa from the website Nikita linked me.

My grandma and grandpa.

Suddenly, my feet feel glued to the ground. Is this a good idea? All the conversation openers I've practiced seem to instantly shrivel in my brain.

"Aimee?" Junho says. "Is this it?"

I shake my head to snap myself out of it. "Yeah. Um. I'm so sorry, I know it's raining, but would you mind if I went in by myself? I think I need to talk to them alone."

I'm so grateful that Junho was willing to come with me, but I'm realizing now that whatever I have to say to my grandparents, I want to do it privately. He hesitates for a second as if unsure about leaving me alone here, but then he nods in understanding.

"I'm going to go find us some umbrellas," he says, shielding his face from the rain with one hand. "I'll meet you back out here, okay?"

I nod and he jogs off.

Okay, Aimee. You can do this.

I take a deep breath and enter the flower shop.

". . . even if you don't like it, you have to go. The yoga will help your back," Halmeoni is saying as she arranges a bouquet.

"Yes, yes, I know, and I will," Harabeoji grumbles from

behind the cash register. He looks up when I enter. "Eseo oseyo. How can we help you?"

The inside of the shop is warm, all light-yellow walls with the smell of lilies and lavender in the air. I clench my fists tight, nails digging into my palms. *Don't disappear. Not now.* I look between the two of them. Harabeoji is tall, with a stooped back and thinning hair. And Halmeoni . . . she looks exactly like my mom, only older, with wrinkled lines around her forehead and graying hair tied into a bun.

For a moment, I can't speak. This is too strange.

"Student?" Halmeoni says. "How can we help you?"

"Oh. Yes. Annyeonghaseyo." I bow hastily and straighten up, realize I'm still clutching the bag of strawberry milk under my jacket. I pull it out and take out the cartons, placing them on the counter. "These are for you."

Halmeoni and Harabeoji exchange glances.

"Um, thank you?" Halmeoni says. "Are you a volunteer of some sort?"

"No." I swallow hard. "I'm Baek Youngmi's daughter."

For a split second, I'm horrified that I've made a terrible mistake. That they're not my grandparents at all. But then both their faces freeze instantly and I know. Halmeoni drops the lily she's holding and presses a hand against her mouth, almost like a movie scene. Harabeoji recovers faster, moving around the counter to take a closer look at me.

"You're Roh Hyunwoo's girl? What's your name?" he asks.

I wince. He doesn't even know my name? I get a sinking feeling in my stomach. I never heard much about my grandparents growing up, but was it the same the other way around? Did they even know I exist?

But no. They must know if they know my dad. "I'm Aimee," I say. "Roh Aimee."

"Wow. Mani keotda," Halmeoni says, taking me in. There's a hint of softness in her eyes as she looks at me. I wonder how she knows how much I've grown if she's never seen me before, but she answers before I can ask myself. "We've only seen pictures of you as a baby and you're a young lady now. Just wait one second."

She disappears into the back of the store and comes out a moment later with a package of Lotus Biscoff Cookies, pressing it into my hand.

"Sorry, this is all we have. I wish we had more food to give you, look how skinny you are! And oh my, you're soaked from the rain."

I feel my cheeks flush. I know it's normal for older Korean people to fuss over you and comment on how much you're eating, but the familiarity feels strange between us. As if we have a relationship. Which we do. But we also don't. Not really.

"Thank you," I say. "I don't want to take up too much of your time."

"How did you find us here?" Harabeoji asks.

"The, um, internet," I say. It doesn't feel like the place

to explain Nikita's master detective work. "I'm in Korea for spring break."

"Is your dad here too?" he asks, glancing at the door as if expecting Appa to burst through at any moment.

"He's here. Well, not here here. He's not at the flower shop. But he's in Gwangju with me."

I'm rambling. They both look at me expectantly like they're waiting for me to say more, to explain what the hell I'm doing here, arriving unannounced. I suddenly feel at a loss for words. Everything feels too weighty, too raw. The temptation to just eat my Lotus biscuit and stick to small talk is overwhelming.

But no. I came here for a reason. I need to do this.

"I wanted to come by and say hello while I'm in town . . ."

"Yes, yes, it's good to see you," Halmeoni says. "Tell your dad we hope he's well."

" . . . and I was wondering if you know where my mom might be," I continue.

They look at each other. The atmosphere feels physically heavier, as if I can feel it pressing into me, squeezing my lungs. Halmeoni is the first to look away, but she doesn't say anything. Harabeoji shifts his gaze to me and smiles tightly.

"We keep in touch. She's well," he says.

Nothing more, nothing less. "Is she also in Gwangju?" I ask.

"She's . . . nearby."

Nearby? Like in the same city nearby or lost somewhere in a memory nearby? Their answers are so curt, I don't know what to say next. The front door opens and a gust of cold air blows in as a man enters, folding up his umbrella.

"Here to pick up a bouquet for Hong Chulsoo?" he says.

"Yes, we have that ready!" Halmeoni says, a little too eagerly.

She and Harabeoji bustle around the shop, ringing up the bouquet for the customer. I stand off to the side, frustration pounding against my chest. I've come this far. There has to be a way for me to get something out of this conversation.

The man takes his bouquet and leaves. I turn to my grandparents.

"I would really like to talk to her if I can," I say. "I know it's been a long time, but I've come all the way here from Vancouver. If there's any way—"

"You can't talk to her," Harabeoji says, cutting me off.

I stare at him. "Why?"

He doesn't explain. Halmeoni chews on her lip, hands clasped together. "It's not that you can't talk to her per se," she says carefully. "It's just that it would be very difficult for that to happen. She's—"

"Yeobo," Harabeoji says sternly, a warning look in his eyes.

Halmeoni presses her lips together. What is going on? Why are they being so elusive?

My phone dings with a message.

Appa:

What time are you and Junho coming back?

I shove it back in my pocket. "Please, I just want to know—"

The door opens again and another customer enters. Then another. Halmeoni and Harabeoji busy themselves with helping them, running back and forth behind the counter. With so many people filling the shop and the rain pounding outside, it's getting so humid in here. I unzip my jacket, feeling bothered all over. It's not just from the humidity. It's the sinking realization that they're not going to tell me anything. The frustration builds in my throat. I came all the way here, and for what?

My phone dings again and I put it on silent without looking at the screen. I walk up to the counter and pick up one of their business cards, flipping it over. I take a pen from the cup next to the cash register and write my phone number, sliding it across the counter to Harabeoji.

"I'm going to leave now because it looks busy," I say. "But if you're willing to talk to me, please give me a call. I'll be leaving town tonight."

It takes all my effort to keep my voice controlled. Harabeoji looks at me, as if sizing me up.

"All right," he says.

But Halmeoni doesn't speak. She's staring intently at my jacket. No, not my jacket. My camera, hanging around my neck, a flicker of recognition in her eyes.

"Hold on," she says. For a moment, I think she's changed her mind about telling me about my mom. But then she disappears again to the back and comes out this time with three more packages of Lotus Biscoff Cookies. She stuffs them in my hands.

"Take care," she says. She holds my hands in hers for a moment and then lets go.

I weave through the customers in the shop and leave, pockets full of biscuits and feeling utterly dissatisfied.

The way Halmeoni and Harabeoji looked at each other and kept things so vague. They're hiding something, I'm sure of it.

But what?

Twenty-Three

Junho's not back yet when I step outside. I wait for him for a minute, pacing down the sidewalk, but it feels like my heart is going to burst and I need to get out of here right now.

I shoot him a quick text.

I don't wait for an answer before getting away from the flower shop as fast as I possibly can.

I'm getting drenched by rain, but I don't care. I pull my jacket tighter around my shoulders and walk with my head down, people with umbrellas passing me on either side. I let my feet carry me, turning right and then left and then left again with no semblance of where I'm actually going. Eventually, I end up at a garden park of some sort and I slow down, my breathing ragged from walking so fast.

My wet hair clings to my face. I stand in the garden and realize I'm shaking.

I don't know what I was expecting from that meeting. Maybe it was my fault, the estranged grandchild showing up unannounced at their workplace. Maybe I should have called first. Maybe it was neither the time nor the place to be asking questions about my mom.

But it's never the time or the place and it feels like everyone who knew her either has nothing to say or nothing they're willing to say to me. Why are there so many secrets surrounding her?

My frustration turns to anger turns to numbness. The rain begins to let up into a shower and I start walking again. I check my phone to see if Junho saw my message. He has, and he's sent one back.

Junho:

Are you okay? Where are you?

There's also the message I got at the flower shop that I didn't look at. That one's from Appa.

Appa:

It's raining a lot. Did you take an umbrella?

I start to type a response to Junho and then backspace, deleting the whole thing. I don't know what to say. I don't want him to worry but at the same time, it feels so exhausting to reply, to try to put this into words.

I keep typing and backspacing as I walk by a rose bush. Dozens of them. I inhale, roses and rain, the smells of flowers and earth and wet pavement.

Describe what it feels like to disappear in ten words or less.

This time it's seamless.

In a blink of an eye, I'm no longer in the garden. I'm standing out on the balcony in my Vancouver apartment. A younger me is there too, six again, leaning over the railing with her hand in the air, trying to catch raindrops.

"Aimee, come in!" my mom calls from inside. "You'll catch a cold standing out there."

Memory Me runs in, leaving the door open. I follow her.

This time, I don't feel like I'm tilting. I don't need to take an inventory of everything around me to situate myself. I just follow, feeling blank inside.

"Umma, I'm so bored," Memory Me whines. "You promised we'd go to the park today."

"It's raining, Aimee." My mom is sitting at the kitchen table, arranging a vase of white roses. She seems to be in a good mood, or at least a calm one. She looks at ease, serene even. Memory Me sits down across from her, watching with her chin in her hands.

"Why do you always buy flowers for yourself?" she asks.

"I like flowers," my mom says.

Memory Me wrinkles her nose. "They smell strong."

"But nice, right?"

"I guess so." Memory Me sighs. "I'm so, *so* bored. When is Appa coming home?"

My mom puts down the roses. For a moment, she looks at a loss for what to do. Then her eyes drift to the kitchen counter and she says, "Do you want cereal?"

There are several boxes of cereal lined up next to each other on the counter. Lucky Charms, Rice Krispies, Honey Nut Cheerios, Frosted Flakes.

"I already had some with Appa this morning," Memory Me says.

A flash of hurt crosses my mom's face, like she's been rejected. "Well, how about a game, then?"

"What kind of game?"

She thinks. "Organize the cereal boxes."

Memory Me shakes her head. "That doesn't sound like a game."

"It is." She gets up, moves to the counter. "Which of these mascots is your favorite?"

"Toucan Sam," Memory Me says immediately.

My mom moves the Froot Loops to the farthest right. "And then after that?"

"The Cheerios bee."

She moves the Honey Nut Cheerios next to the Froot Loops. "Can I move the next one?" Memory Me asks.

My mom nods. I watch the two of them rank the rest of

the cereal boxes and then reorganize them alphabetically. Then by color. Then by favorite overall flavor. It was the beginning of the cereal library, as my mom coined it. I stand by the balcony, watching them, listening to the rain in the background. It's nice. Cozy. A memory I didn't even remember having.

And then I blink and I'm back in the garden.

No. Not yet. That was too short. I don't want to be back here yet, don't want to process everything that just happened and everything I don't know. I want to be back in a time that was simpler, when I knew exactly where my mom was. In the kitchen, organizing cereal boxes with me.

I close my eyes and breathe deep, focusing on the smells and the memory. Rain and roses, roses and rain.

When I open my eyes, I'm on the balcony again.

"Aimee, come in! You'll catch a cold standing out there."

I go in.

This time when they organize the cereal boxes, I get closer. When my mom asks Memory Me who her favorite mascot is, I answer too, even though no one can hear me.

"It's Tony the Tiger now," I say. "Don't worry, you grow up and realize he's actually the best."

They organize the boxes and the memory ends, sending me back to the garden again.

No. Not yet. I focus, eyes shut tight, swimming in the scents.

"Aimee, come in! You'll catch a cold standing out there."

I go back, again and again, to watch them line up the

cereal boxes. Each time I end up back in the garden, I picture the memory, focus on the smells. Each time, it takes a little less time, a little less concentration for me to go back. I feel almost like I'm in a trance, just following the rhythms of disappearing.

Soon, the memory loops twice without sending me to the garden at all. The whole scene plays out, and then when it's done, I'm on the balcony again, starting from the beginning.

I breathe a sigh of relief. It knows I want to stay so it's letting me.

But then eventually, it sends me to the garden again, but only for a second. Almost as soon as my feet touch the ground and I see the roses, I'm back in the apartment. It happens so fast I feel like I have whiplash.

My head aches, shaking me out of my numbness, my trance. *What am I doing?* I have to get out of here.

I wait for the memory to end and I'm in the garden again.

But then, without me even trying, I blink and I'm back in the apartment.

"Aimee, come in! You'll catch a cold standing out there."

My heart begins to pound in my ears. Okay. It's okay. This is just a mistake. I just have to wait it out. I tap my fingers against the counter, trying to stay calm. This is no big deal.

But when the memory ends, it starts again at the balcony, replaying itself.

"Aimee, come in! You'll catch a cold standing out there."

I breathe in through my nose, out through my mouth. Panic starts to creep in, making my hands feel clammy. I wipe them against my pants, which are still wet from the rain. They do nothing to help.

The memory ends and to my great relief, I'm back in the garden. But my head is throbbing now and I can feel it—the pull. My vision flickers and for half a second I see the apartment and then the garden again. Apartment then garden, apartment then garden, like I'm switching between two channels on TV.

"Are you okay?" an unfamiliar voice yells, startling me. My vision stops splitting and the garden solidifies in front of me. A kid holding a yellow umbrella is standing there, staring at me.

"Are you a video game character?" he asks. "Why are you glitching like that?"

I feel majorly disoriented, even more than I usually do coming back from a memory. A thick fog clouds my mind and I shake my head, trying to clear it. "What time is it?"

The kid looks at the big plastic watch on his wrist. "Almost 12:30 p.m."

I look at my phone. It says 11:21 a.m.

Was I going back and forth like that for almost an hour?

I thank the kid and leave before he can ask more questions. The rain has slowed to a mild drizzle now and the sun is starting to peek out through the clouds, but my teeth are still chattering from the cold. Or maybe it's from the shock.

What *was* that? That's never happened to me before. It's almost like I was . . .

No. It was just a one-off thing. Nothing to worry about. I'm just extra tired and stressed today, which probably made it worse. It will never happen again.

But even as I reassure myself, I can't ignore the uneasiness spreading through my chest, cold and unyielding.

I shake my head and hurry along.

KAKAO MESSENGER

Junho:

Aimee? Just checking in. I know you said you needed some time to yourself, but my dad is telling me to come back now and I'm not sure what to tell him. Do you think you'll come back soon?

Junho:

Okay, so I see that you're not seeing any of my messages. Trying to keep my cool here and convince myself that you've very likely not been kidnapped in an unfamiliar city haha . . .

Junho:

Maybe your phone died?

Junho:

Btw, here's a link for a great portable charger, in case you're in the market for one!

Appa:

Aimee? Are you getting my messages?

Appa:

~~I'm getting worried.~~ Message deleted.

Appa:

Call me when you see this.

Twenty-Four

I restart my phone, trying to orient myself. I don't know where I am or what I'm doing. I need to open Naver Maps and figure out how to get back to the Airbnb.

My phone resets and I see I have a missed call. Dozens of missed calls and texts actually, from Appa and Junho, but there's also one call from an unknown number and a string of voice mails. I sit down on a bench at the opposite end of the garden and press listen, trying to gather myself.

"Hey, Aimee, it's Junho," Junho's voice says. "I'm starting to freak out. Are you okay? Where did you go? I'm back with my dad and your dad now and I just told them that you'll be out a little longer, but I think they're starting to get suspicious. Let me know that you're safe, okay?"

Beep. Next message.

"Aimee, where are you?" Appa's voice says. "Call me back immediately."

Beep. Next message.

"Hi, Aimee, this is Halmeoni from the flower shop," Halmeoni's voice says. I sit up straighter. "I'm sorry about earlier. I feel bad about how you left and, well, if you'd like to talk more, please come back to the flower shop tonight at closing. We close at 4:00 p.m. I will be here."

End of messages.

I replay the last one.

Halmeoni is willing to talk to me. I feel hopeful and skeptical all at once, but mostly, I don't know how to feel. This is a second chance, though. I have to take it.

I still have a few hours to kill before 4:00 p.m. I hesitate, looking at the unanswered texts from Junho and Appa on my phone.

I hate to leave them hanging, but it's only for a few more hours. For now, I just send a quick text to Junho only.

Me:

> Hey I'm safe! No need to worry. Just need a bit more time, I'll be back later today.

I'll catch up with them properly right after I talk to Halmeoni. Sharing more details now would only invite more questions and they'll probably want me to join them right away. It's easier to stay MIA for a little bit longer than to have to slip away again.

"I'm sorry," I say quietly to the screen before turning off my phone and tucking it back into my pocket.

It's 4:00 p.m.

For a few hours, I wandered, passing through a marketplace selling grains and produce, several cafés, a row of boutique independent clothing stores, and a gyeran bap restaurant where I stopped to get myself a rice roll wrapped in egg. I ate it with the Lotus Biscoff Cookies. I had zero appetite, but I figured I should probably eat something, anything, before seeing my grandparents for the second time.

It hits me while I make my way back to It's a Good Flower Day that in another scenario, Gwangju would have been a fun place to visit. I imagine an alternate universe me, shopping with Junho, sitting at a café with my journal, visiting museums.

Instead, I find myself in front of the flower shop again. The sandwich board has been taken in and the closed sign hangs in the glass front door, but it's still unlocked, maybe for me. I take a breath and enter.

At first the shop seems totally empty. Then Halmeoni appears from the back, wiping her hands on her apron.

"Annyeonghaseyo." I bow.

"You're here," she says. She gestures for me to come behind the counter. There are two stools and we both take a seat, facing each other.

"Is Harabeoji here?" I ask, peering over her shoulder.

"He goes to yoga class on Wednesdays so I close the shop on my own."

"I see. Does he know you're meeting me?"

She pauses, folding her hands in her lap. This time she

looks me straight in the eye, no hint of the elusiveness from this morning. "No. He thinks it would only hurt you to know the truth. You caught me off guard earlier, but I was thinking after you left and I've made up my mind to tell you what you need to know. You've come all the way here. You should get some answers."

I don't realize I'm holding my breath until my lungs start to ache. I exhale slowly, hands gripping the stool beneath me. "Please tell me where my mom is."

I brace myself for it. *Your mom is missing.*

She's stuck in a time loop.

That's why she left you.

She's been in a memory this whole time trying to get back to you.

But what she says instead is this.

"Your mom's remarried. She's living in Suwon with her husband and two sons."

Time stills. I can't have heard right.

"Nae?" I say. *What?*

The way she looks at me, it makes my stomach sink. It's a look of pity.

"We also weren't sure how much your dad has told you, so we didn't want to say anything," she says. "But if he told you anything of importance, I don't think you would have come to see us today."

She sighs deeply. "It's a long and complicated story between your parents. But the short version is this. They started dating when they were young, and when they were nineteen, they got pregnant by accident. Youngmi didn't know what to do. She had just started university and she wasn't ready to be a mom, but abortions were illegal at the time in South Korea. Even though many people still did it covertly, your mom had conflicting feelings about it. The only thing she knew for sure was that the day she found out, she had been planning to break things off with your father.

"She didn't love him anymore, but without him, she would have to live the life of a single mother, and at such a young age. We told her that was not an option, to be a single mom. It would affect everything—her education, her future career options, every single detail of her life. To be a single mom in Korea is to be an outcast. I told her she cannot be part of our family if she chooses this."

At this, Halmeoni's face lines with guilt. "I only wanted to protect her, to urge her to make the right decision. But I spoke too harshly and was too hard on her for her mistake."

Her mistake. Meaning me. I'm so stunned by the story that I can't do anything but stare, frozen to my seat. I always knew Appa had me at a young age, but I never knew the circumstances, never knew all this.

"She was so angry with me that she chose to leave me first," Halmeoni says, somber. "Harabeoji says I chased her out, and maybe I did, but there were a lot of factors. Your father said he'd marry her, but she said no. She didn't want this life. She was always stubborn, ruthlessly so. All her friends, everyone she knew, judged her for it. So she escaped. Your dad still had his Canadian citizenship from being born there so they decided to leave the country altogether and start fresh.

"They went. They tried. She had the baby in Canada, unmarried, but she was unbearably unhappy there. She knew she was only running away, that this was just a temporary escape, and eventually she decided to come back here and start over. And slowly, she did. She met someone, got married, and has two kids now, and this time, she's actually ready to be a mom."

She looks away and laughs a little, shaking her head. "I suppose the short version was still quite long."

I don't know what to say. How did I never know any of this? I didn't even know Appa and my mom weren't married. I always wondered why I never saw any wedding photos at my house when Nikita's parents had a whole album in theirs. Halmeoni is staring at me, waiting for my response, but my brain feels frozen, like it doesn't know which detail to land on, so it just keeps circling over everything, trying to make sense of it all. Only it doesn't make sense. None of this does.

"Do they know?" I ask. "Her new family. Do they know about me?"

I'm not sure why that's the first question that comes out of my mouth, but suddenly, I need to know. All this time I've been thinking of her, has she been thinking of me too?

Halmeoni looks at the floor. "They do not."

My heart cracks. "You can't just leave your family behind and start a new one like they don't exist."

She looks back up at me and there it is again. Pity.

"Your mom is not a bad person, Aimee. She made mistakes and has deep regrets about the way things happened, but all she wanted was a second chance at life to do things right. And this time, I'm not going to chase her away." She pauses, gesturing to the camera around my neck. "When I saw you with that camera, I saw her again as a teenager. It was like she was standing right in front of me. I'm going to protect her now like I should have done the first time around. Please believe me when I say we have no bad feelings toward you or your dad, but it is better this way for everybody."

Is it better this way for everybody? Is it better this way for me?

"I'm sorry," she says. It sounds like she means it.

There's a part of me that wants to scream, that wants to grab the vases off the display case and shatter them against the floor, shredding every flower in this shop to mulch. And then there's a part of me that wants to curl up and cry until my insides are scraped raw and there's nothing left to cry about.

This isn't how it was supposed to go.

But the biggest part of me is neither screaming nor crying. It's just numb.

It's this part that takes over as if on autopilot, that thanks Halmeoni for her time and rises to say goodbye, that answers when she asks, "When are you going back to Canada?"

"Sunday," I say.

"Take care of yourself, okay?"

It's this numb part of me that swallows every feeling, the rage, the sadness, the shock, and manages to wish her good health as a final parting. "Geonganghaseyo." I bow one last time.

And then I step out of the flower shop, into the rain that's picked up again, and I see a familiar person standing there, holding an umbrella, staring through the glass front door at Halmeoni. And then his gaze turns to me, expression unreadable.

"Appa," I say, my voice cracking.

Twenty-Five

Appa and I sit side by side at a bus stop, but not really. He's here in Gwangju, South Korea, Planet Earth, and I'm on Mars—no, farther, Neptune. He won't even look at me, which is fine because I'm not looking at him either. We orbit past each other silently, all our unspoken words hanging heavy between us.

Everyone was worried about me. After I sent Junho the text telling him that I'm safe, Appa pressed Junho to tell him where he last saw me, and Junho eventually relented. I turned my phone back on to see dozens of texts and missed calls, Junho saying, *Your dad is looking for you, I'm so sorry, I had to tell him.*

Appa and I left the flower shop before Halmeoni could see him. We settle at the bus stop because it's empty and shielded from the rain, but it feels like the wrong place to talk about everything that just happened. Then again, I'm not sure there is a right place.

"Why?" he says finally, breaking the silence. His voice is quiet, but it shatters me as if he's yelling through a megaphone. "Why did you go there?"

I look down at my shoes. Become suddenly fascinated by the scuff marks on my heels.

"What did they tell you?"

I don't say anything. I'm still processing, still too numb.

"Mal an halgeoya?" His voice is frustrated, angry.

The phrase strikes me like a punch in the gut. *You're just not going to talk?* How funny, coming from him, the man who refused to talk to me for years. Suddenly, it's too much to bear and all my pent-up emotions come rushing out, unstoppable and ugly.

"Did you know?" I say. "Did you know she has a new family?"

He presses his lips together, telling me everything I need to know.

I laugh in disbelief. "I can't believe you knew and you never told me. I can't believe that all this time, you said you had no idea why she left, that one day she just packed her bags and decided to leave when you knew all along!"

"What did they tell you?" Appa asks again, his voice louder now, demanding.

"She told me everything! She told me I was an accident that happened when you were young, that my mom didn't want to get married to you, and that she left us because we were never the life she wanted in the first place. She told me everything you didn't."

My voice rises with each word and I realize that I'm shaking. I have never yelled at my dad before. It feels

colossally wrong, and yet, I can't stop myself. It's like I'm totally out of control.

"If you had just told me this from the beginning, I wouldn't have gone looking for her or my grandparents. I would never have found out this way."

"You should have never found out at all!" Now he's yelling too, explosive. I shrink back. I've never seen him so mad. "I never wanted you to know any of this, at least not now, not while you're still a kid. I thought maybe when you got older, then you could know."

"I'm not a kid anymore, Appa."

"You clearly are! Only a kid would do something so foolish like this. Is this why you wanted to come to Korea in the first place? To look for your mom?"

Now it's my turn to press my lips together, looking away.

He shakes his head. "Why did you have to do this? Why did you have to go looking?"

"So this is all my fault?" I say incredulously.

"Then whose fault would it be?" he snaps. "Some things are better left untouched, Aimee. Now that you know all this, did it make things better for you? For anyone? What did you even achieve here?"

"How am I supposed to know? I literally just found out everything right now!"

"You might not know it yet, but I do. We were better off before you did this."

We are orbiting farther and farther away from each

other. Why does he keep blaming me for everything? I'm not the one who abandoned us. I'm not the one who kept him in the dark his whole life. All I wanted was closure so I could live my life with a semblance of normality. I can't even see him anymore. All I see is the bright red glow of the sun, of my hurt and fury and rage.

"Better off? *What* was better off?" I shout. "Let me ask you this, Appa. Why did you even come to Korea? If you wanted to fly all the way out here just to not talk to me, you could have waited for me to come home to do that. It's what we do every single goddamn day anyway. Why waste money on a plane ticket to do it here too? I was having a fine time before you came!"

He looks at me in disbelief and for a second, I think I've hurt him. And then his face shutters, closing off completely.

"This was a mistake," he says, his voice flat. "I should have never come here."

I press the heels of my hands against my eyes, trying to gain control again, breathing shakily. "I'm sorry. I didn't mean it."

"No. It's fine." He rises, hands in his pockets. "I'm going home."

"I'll go with you—" I start to stand, gathering my things.

"Not to the Airbnb. To Vancouver."

I still. "What? You can't be serious."

"You're right. You were fine before I came here, and these are all things we can talk about at home. So you finish up the trip with Mr. Kim and Junho and I'll see you when you come back." He doesn't look at me the whole time he talks. Instead, he places his umbrella on the bench next to me and starts to walk away.

"You're leaving?" I say to his back. "Just like that?"

And he does.

He leaves.

Just like that.

Twenty-Six

By the time I get back to the Airbnb, Appa has already packed up his things and left for the KTX to go back to Seoul. Junho and Mr. Kim look relieved to see me, but entirely perplexed. Appa must have given the bare minimum of an explanation before he left.

"Are you okay?" Junho asks. "What happened?"

How do I even begin? I don't know what to say so I just say I'm fine. There's a mix of feelings in his eyes—confusion, a little bit of hurt, a look that says he doesn't believe me—but he lets it go for now and says nothing.

The ride to Busan is quiet.

Mr. Kim plays no music and I stare out the window the whole time. I can't make sense of this. Of anything.

I see my mom in my head, roses at the kitchen table, organizing cereal boxes with me. I see us on the beach with our hodu gwaja, clinking them together in cheers.

How could she have left us the way that Halmeoni said she did? How could she have left me?

I think again of the woman in white, the one I saw in my memory. The other time traveler. It could still be her.

274

Just because she has a new family doesn't mean she doesn't also have STWS. It doesn't mean she's not still visiting me at least through her memories.

You're being naive, I think to myself.

Maybe. But I need to know for sure.

We arrive in Busan and settle in for the night. Junho and Mr. Kim order us fried chicken delivery for dinner and I start to map out the beginnings of a plan.

"Mani meogeo, Aimee," Mr. Kim says, piling my plate with the biggest drumsticks.

Junho arranges the side dishes on the table, cabbage salad with sesame dressing and white radish cut into cubes, putting them all closest to me. They're pretending everything is normal to try to lighten the mood, to try to cheer me up. Their kindness makes me want to cry.

"My dad and I will be visiting family tomorrow," Junho says as we eat. "Do you want to come with us?"

Right. Tomorrow was supposed to be Junho and Mr. Kim's family day, and my day alone with Appa. So much for father-daughter bonding.

I shake my head. "It's okay. I think I'll just rest here, if that's fine with you both. Maybe go for a walk to the beach."

Mr. Kim looks worried. "By yourself?"

"I'll have my phone with me. And it'll be on the whole time," I add.

Well, mostly the whole time.

Junho opens his mouth like he wants to protest and then

closes it again, looking helpless. Mr. Kim reluctantly agrees. We finish up dinner and go to bed. When I close my eyes, I see the look on Appa's face before he walked away from me, and I sleep, restless.

Our Airbnb is close to Gwangalli Beach. It faces Gwangan Bridge, which supposedly lights up at night, but when I go, it's still daytime. It's not raining today, but the sky is overcast and the air is chilly so there aren't many people at the beach. Just like I was hoping.

I choose a particularly secluded spot and lay my towel on the sand. I sit down, tucking my knees into my chest, and stare out to the water. Being so close to it makes me feel like I'm home again, in Vancouver. There's a comfort to it that eases the ache in my chest I've been feeling since yesterday. Since everything.

The breeze whips my hair back. I close my eyes, inhale deep, focus on the smell of the ocean.

It's a different scent from the walnuts and red bean that took me back before, but I think it could still work. It could still be connected enough.

Sand and sea and salty waters. I picture Kitsilano.

When I open my eyes again, I'm there.

Memory Me and my mom are eating their hodu gwaja. I watch as my mom's eyes fill with tears, as Appa runs over and takes her hand.

"Jib eh gago shipeo," she says.

"We can do that," Appa says. "We can go home right now. Aimee, pack your things."

"No." My mom shakes her head and repeats, "Jib eh gago shipeo. My real home."

The words have new meaning now, knowing what she meant. She wanted to go back home to Korea. Not just Korea. If it was only a matter of place, maybe we could have all gone back together. She wanted to go back to the life she originally wanted, the one that didn't include me and Appa in her future.

But it's hard to understand how she could have been so okay with it, especially seeing Memory Me sitting there right next to her. I was her child. How could she forget me so easily?

I swallow the lump in my throat and stand up, dusting the sand off my black pants and walking toward the shoreline. I wait for the woman.

Please appear. Please.

She doesn't and the memory ends.

I'm back at Gwangalli Beach again. I exhale slowly. I will do this for as long as it takes.

I restart my phone, checking for messages to make sure that this time, I don't worry Junho or Mr. Kim. There are none and I close my eyes again, concentrating on the scent. The beach. The memory.

I go back.

"Umma's hodu gwaja must taste bad," Memory Me says.

I head for the shore.

I keep doing this again and again until, just like that time in the rose garden, the memory starts to loop by itself without me returning to the present. It replays two times, three times, four before sending me back to Busan, where I stay long enough only to check my phone before vanishing again.

Hours pass. But this time, I'm not scared. I stay determined, watching the scene over and over, walking along the shoreline. I take in more details each time. The people on the paddleboards look like twins, one teaching the other how to paddle without falling. There are five teenagers in the water, hollering over who can swim the farthest. As the others dive underwater, one of the girls pulls another of the girls to the side and kisses her on the lips. They smile at each other, the tide rolling against their arms.

Behind them all, a daughter and father make turtles in the sand. I try not to look at them.

And then, almost like a miracle, I see her.

She appears as if from nowhere, popping into the memory from thin air. The woman in white, only today she's not wearing white at all, but a gray sweater with jeans, her back turned to me so I can't yet see her face.

For a second, I think I must be imagining it. That I just wanted to see her so badly I'm hallucinating. I rub my eyes, but no. She's still there.

I run, heart beating wildly.

"Excuse me!" I call. "Excuse me!"

She turns, slowly, a shocked look on her face.

My breath catches. My heart bursts.

It's her, but it's not *her*.

The woman who turns is a stranger, a face I've never seen before.

"How do you see me?" she asks, bewildered.

Disappointment crushes me, a fist clenching tight in my ribs as I slow down to a walk, coming to a stop in front of her. I know it was unlikely. I know it was a long shot. I know I know I know. But the truth guts me in a way that makes me realize that as much as I knew, I was hoping against it, hoping for an impossible thing.

"I have STWS," I say. "This is my memory."

The woman is Asian, but she looks younger than my mom would currently be, and she looks completely different now that I can see her clearly. She nods in understanding.

"I see. I've never met another traveler before, but I heard it can happen." Her eyes widen. "Actually, I think I heard you last time I was visiting this memory. Did you call out to me?"

"Yes." I swallow hard. "I thought you might be someone else."

She smiles apologetically. "Sorry."

"It's okay. It's not your fault."

She points out to the water at the two teen girls. "This was where my wife and I had our first kiss. Sometimes when I see the ocean, I come back here."

"That's a nice memory to visit."

"What about you?"

I point to the sand where Memory Me is sitting. "That's me as a child. I was here with my parents."

"That's also nice."

"Yeah," I say, for lack of better words. How strange it is that someone could be having one of the best moments of their lives just steps away from where someone else is falling apart. That at the very same beach where my mom was crying for home, two teen girls were finding home in each other. "Are you still in Vancouver?" I ask.

"I just recently moved back after living abroad," she says. "Are you?"

"Yes."

"Have you heard of the Vancouver STWS meetups?" she asks. "I just started going and it's been nice."

I manage a smile. "I think I've heard of that before."

"You should come check it out," she says. "Oh, I think my time is almost up. Here comes my brother."

Sure enough, the teenage boy I saw the first time I came here comes running toward the water, barreling right through the woman like she's not even there.

"I hope we meet again," she says, and then she disappears.

I lift a hand and wave at the spot where she stood. Then I slowly lower my hand and walk back across the sand to Memory Me, my heart growing heavy again.

All this time, I thought my mom might be trying to make her way back to me. That maybe we had a special connection, that all my disappearances lately were a sign for me to make my way back to her too. Now I realize how far-fetched, how foolish that was. There were no signs.

It wasn't her.

It was never her.

And now I'm all alone.

Twenty-Seven

Describe how it feels to disappear in ten words or less.

It's something like this: the line blurs with reality, too faded to see straight.

What is the memory? What is the present?

I curl up in the sand, staring at the water. Memory Me builds turtles around me and then the turtles vanish and she's back on the beach towel, eating hodu gwaja. The scene loops over and over, and every so often, Busan will flicker in my vision for a second before disappearing again. I'm not even sure which beach I'm looking at sometimes.

Busan.

Vancouver.

Gwangalli.

Kitsilano.

It all blends together.

The memory keeps looping and I let it. I'm too tired to fight, to do anything but lie here in the sand.

And to think, this all started because I wanted to stop disappearing. Because I thought finding my mom would help me find closure, would maybe even help me feel less alone. That somehow, my memories might even be leading me to her.

I laugh and then the laughter turns to tears, coursing down my face. I cry until my body aches, until I have no more tears left to cry. And then I yell into the sky, angry and loud. No one can hear me here so I yell even louder, louder and louder, until my throat feels raw.

When I met the Hapjeong Station Ghost, I didn't understand why someone might want to succumb to a time loop. But now I think it must be because here, you don't have to hold anything back. You don't have to pretend to be okay.

I sit up from the sand, feeling empty.

What would happen if I just stayed here?

"Look, Aimee, I made a turtle," Appa says to Memory Me. "You can name him."

"I want to name him Alex!" Memory Me shouts.

There's a sharpness in my chest looking at my younger self. She doesn't know yet that she's going to be abandoned. That she's going to start disappearing. That she's going to feel lost. If I stay in the memory, she'll never be hurt again. It will just be the same routine, predictable, easy for me to protect her forever.

I look down at my hands, at the faded pear on my wrist that Junho drew, still hanging on. I took care to wash around it so it wouldn't get erased and I cling to it now, fingers pressed against my skin.

If I stay here, she'll be safe. But she'll never have more firsts.

I wanted to stop disappearing so I could live my life, but even with the vanishing, there were still firsts, weren't there? First time admiring the plum blossoms. First time walking through a green tea field. First meetup that made me feel like I belonged, first road trip in Korea, first boy who made my heart race.

Memory Me beams. I reach out to her, my fingers passing through her shoulder.

She deserves more. I thought finding my mom would give that to her, but maybe I can do it instead.

I wipe my eyes. I need to get out of here.

But the memory restarts again and I don't know what to do. I sit by the water and close my eyes, take a deep inhale. Maybe I can return to the present the way I arrived in the past. Through smell. I breathe in the scent of sea and sand, but when I open my eyes again, I'm still here. I try one more time, this time picturing Gwangalli Beach as clearly as I can.

But it doesn't work. The memory only loops again.

Panic starts to creep in. It gets harder to breathe. "Please," I whisper, closing my eyes.

I open them. Still here.

I try, over and over. There's a moment when I appear back on my beach towel in Busan, but as soon as I register it, I'm gone again. There's not enough time to grasp on to the present, and every time I do come back to it, it keeps slipping loose from my hands.

Oh god.

I start to feel sick.

I'm stuck in the time loop.

It's even worse this time than at the rose garden. I'm certain that hours have passed. What if Junho and Mr. Kim are trying to reach me? They're almost definitely trying to reach me. Shit. Shit shit shit. How could I have let this happen?

I hold my head between my knees and try to breathe. It's going to be okay. I'm going to get out of this. Stay calm.

One sense at a time. The advice from the forums comes back to me, an old anchor that I grasp on to now. *Going back to a memory can be disorienting. Name where you are one sense at a time to ground yourself.*

What do you hear?

"Look, Aimee, I made a turtle," Appa says to Memory Me. "You can name him."

I look up at Appa and it hits me then how young he is. He was nineteen when he found out he was going to have a baby. That's only a couple of years older than I am right now. I can't believe he moved to Vancouver, had a child, and tried to build a life for his new family at that age.

The memory restarts.

I swallow down my panic. *What do you see?*

I get up, and this time, I follow Appa instead of Memory

Me or my mom. I watch as he gathers water in the pail, as he turns to see my mom crying, as he runs over as fast as he can. There's a gentleness to the way he talks to her, but also a pain in his eyes that I didn't notice before, a deep exhaustion like he's at a loss for what to do.

I notice the way he distracts Memory Me from the way my mom withdraws from us by turning my attention to the sandcastles. He's trying so hard and I feel such a mix of emotions watching him.

"I'm mad at you," I say, standing right next to him as he builds his sandcastle. "I'm mad at you for keeping so much from me. I'm mad at you for leaving me in Gwangju. I'm mad at you for not listening when I said I needed help."

My voice is hoarse from tears. He doesn't hear a word.

"I'm mad at you for trying so hard," I say. "Why are you doing that? She leaves us anyway. She doesn't stay."

"Look, Aimee, I made a turtle," he says.

He looks so proud, it breaks my heart. And I realize that these are all words I need to be saying to present-day Appa. Not this Appa in the memory.

I sit back down and close my eyes, but this time instead of picturing Gwangalli Beach, I picture Appa in the present day. I picture him turning away from me at the bus stop, playing Jay-Z in the car, showing up at Gomo's apartment with his suitcase and cantaloupe luggage tag. I picture returning to him, and when I open my eyes, I'm in Busan.

But it's only for three seconds. Even before I disappear

again, I can feel how little time I have, like the past has one hand on my shoulder, ready to pull me back at any moment. I'm gone again before I can even touch my phone.

Focus. I take a deep breath, picture Appa, think of all the things I need to say to him.

Slowly, I return to Busan for longer and longer stretches of time. Five seconds. Seven seconds. Ten. It still slips through my fingers, the memory tugging me back like the time loop itself has gotten stronger. But I resist, pulling against it.

Gwangalli gets longer. Kitsilano gets shorter.

Gwangan Bridge appears before me. It's lit up in rainbow colors against the night sky.

I count, my head throbbing. Two. Five. Ten. I'm still here, but I feel almost seasick, like I might disappear again at any moment. I look down at my hands, see that they're still glitching. Please no. Please let me stay.

I grab my phone and restart it, hands shaking so hard I drop it. I frantically scoop it back up as the screen flashes with the time: 10:12 p.m. I've been looping in and out all day.

I don't know how much time I have. I ignore all the notifications on my phone and call Appa.

He picks up immediately. "Aimee?" His voice is urgent. "Where are you?"

"Appa, I need to talk to you. I need to tell you that I'm mad at you."

"Where are you?"

"Gwangalli Beach. But Appa, I need to tell you—"

"I'm coming. Appa's coming. I'm at Gwangalli too."

"You what? You are?"

"Where at the beach are you? I'm—"

The call cuts off as I vanish again.

"No!" I yell.

But I'm not gone entirely, not this time. I'm still glitching as if living one minute in the past, one minute in the present, back and forth, neither here nor there.

The sea in the night.

The sea in the day.

My mom, lifting the hodu gwaja to her lips with a smile.

Appa, trying to hold our family together like water to sand.

Me, the girl at the edge of the world.

Busan.

Vancouver.

Busan.

Vancouver.

And then, just as I reappear: Appa in the present, standing in front of me, reaching out to grab my hand.

Twenty-Eight

"**S**tay with me, Aimee, I'm here."

Appa grips my hand tight and I cling to him back, knees shaking, so confused.

"Appa? What are you doing here? I thought you went to Seoul," I say.

"I did, but I took the KTX to Busan today. Here, drink this."

He pulls a water bottle from a plastic bag around his arm. We sit down on the beach towel and I drink. My hands are still glitching and Appa stares, brow furrowed, but doesn't say anything. He just reaches into the bag and pulls out a scarf, wrapping it around my neck.

"You have to stay warm," he says. "You're shaking."

"Thanks." I start to feel a little less nauseous and a little more solid, like I'm here again, really here. I take a deep breath and look into Appa's bag. "What's all this?"

Inside, there are boxes of strawberry Pepero sticks, Yakult drinks, and milk buns. "I read that eating and staying warm helps people who come back from an STWS-triggered memory," he says. "Eat this."

He stuffs a bun in my hands. I'm suddenly reminded of the buns we used to get when I was a kid, lining up just so I could collect the stickers tucked in each package.

"You read about STWS?" I ask.

"On the train. Hold on one second."

His phone is ringing inside his pocket and he answers. "Hello? Yes, I found her. She's okay. We'll be back in a bit. Okay, okay. Thanks, Hyung. Thank you." He hangs up and turns to me. "That was Mr. Kim. Junho says hi."

"Oh my god." I shake my head, embarrassment flaring in my cheeks. "I can't believe I did this to them."

"Don't worry. They'll be okay." He goes quiet, looking out at the lit-up Gwangan Bridge, casting a neon glow into the water. "You said on the phone that you're mad at me?"

"So mad," I say.

I think of all the words I said to Appa in the memory, but now that he's actually in front of me to hear it, I feel at a loss for words. I turn to him, clutching the water bottle and bun in my hands, no longer glitching.

"But first I want to tell you how it feels to disappear. And I'm going to use lots of words, more than ten of them. And you have to listen to all of it, okay?"

He looks at me and he nods.

"It feels like always being on guard, like you never know what's going to be the thing that sends you over. You have to get used to living your life with these huge interruptions, and it's so disorienting that all of your energy goes to anticipating them, as if that'll stop it from happening. But it doesn't and you're just tired all the time. It feels like never living in the moment because you don't know when the moment will be stolen from you. So you go numb instead and tell yourself you're fine.

"Sometimes it's not so bad. It's even kind of nice when the memory is a good one. But sometimes it's even worse than what you could have imagined and you start to think you're losing your mind, that nobody can help you. That maybe the only person who might is someone who's not even there, so you start to make these elaborate plans to find them and you fool yourself into believing they might be trying to find you too."

My voice cracks. "I wish you told me the truth sooner. And I wish you listened to me when I said I needed you. Not just lately, but ever since she left. Because after she was gone, I feel like you left me too. It was slower and quieter, but you left me behind in a different kind of way. And I don't know how to find you again even though you're right in front of me."

Appa is looking at me intently, tears filling his eyes. "Aimee, Appa ga jalmotaesseo. I made a mistake. I'm sorry. Appa is really sorry."

I'm crying now, and he is too. It's my second time ever seeing Appa cry.

"I just wanted to protect you," he says. "Specialists, therapy . . . it's all not something I know very well. I can't help but be wary of it, like they'll try and convince you that there's something wrong with you."

"Appa, there's nothing wrong with needing some help," I say, wiping my tears away. "There's no shame in admitting that."

He sighs deeply. "I just grew up differently."

"I know. Gomo tried to explain a little bit to me."

Appa nods, falling silent and staring down at his hands. Then he turns to face me again. "Do you know what convinced me to come to Korea?"

I shake my head.

"Gomo said that if I don't make efforts now, I'm going to lose you. That you're going to keep on growing up and drifting farther and farther away from me and one day, I'm going to look around and I won't know how to close the distance between us anymore." He looks down at his hands and then back up at me. "I'm sorry I didn't tell you the truth about your mom. I promise I did mean to one day. I just didn't want to hurt you. And I'm sorry I left Gwangju yesterday the way that I did. I had so many regrets about that when I woke up this morning, I decided to head to Busan right away."

"Where you discovered I was missing again?" I say.

"If Mr. Kim wasn't already bald, all his hair would have been falling out from stress," Appa says seriously. "Luckily, they said you mentioned walking at the beach, so that's where I went looking."

I imagine Appa wandering around the beach, going back and forth for hours to find me. I wrap the scarf tighter around myself, the tide drifting in and out, lapping up against the sand. "What did you think?" I ask quietly. "When she got pregnant?" From what I learned, it was the thing that derailed my mom's life. I need to know if Appa felt the same, if maybe he still does.

"It was the best news of my life," he says.

My eyebrows rise, suspicious. "Really?"

"Well, maybe not at first. It was a mix of things. I was surprised and scared but also excited. And then it was tough to see how distraught it made your mom. You have to understand, she was always very complicated. She was never just one thing. Some days, she would talk about giving the baby up for adoption, other days she was certain she could make it work one way or another. She had very good days and very bad days, sometimes in the span of one hour, always disappearing into her mind. I told her that no matter what, I would be there for her and for our child. But I was also terrified of becoming a dad."

He gets a distant look in his eyes, but this time it doesn't make him feel far away. This time he invites me with him. "Neither of us were perfect people. But even so, I knew I would love this baby more than anything in the world. And when you arrived in the world, it was true. That's why it was the best news."

"Even though it made you lose her?"

The thought has been in my mind since yesterday. That if it wasn't for me, things might have worked out differently for Appa and my mom.

He grips my hand, holding tight. "Never think that. It was a difficult situation and she made her decisions. We both did. Besides." He smiles sadly. "Just because you thought someone was the love of your life doesn't mean you were the love of theirs."

I nod, believing him, and hold his hand back tight. "Okay," I say. "Okay."

We sit like that for a long time, holding hands like we'll sink if we don't. It's freezing cold, but neither of us moves. I still have so many questions, about my mom, about my dad, about all the silent moments between us. As it turns out, Appa and I are alike in more ways than I thought. This whole time, we were both trying to get back to each other, getting caught again and again in the space between here and now until finally, we arrived, both feet planted on the ground. So for now, I let the questions rest.

For now, I simply stay where I am.

On the page with the stickers from Blue Bunny Bakery. Added: a cutout of the milk bun wrapper and Pepero box. Someone has drawn a rabbit on both cutouts, wearing a bread hat. Writing underneath: Snacks from Appa, illustrations from Junho (not part of the official collection but maybe even better). Full twelve-sticker set now complete.

Twenty-Nine

Gamcheon Culture Village is a maze of colorful houses stacked on a hillside. The stairs are steep and the street art is brilliant, murals spilling out in every direction. I race down the winding alleyway, twisting and turning, stopping to call behind my shoulder, "Junho! Hurry up!"

"Aimee, this may shock you, but you know the village won't pick up and leave if we're too slow, right?" he says, trying to keep up with me. "We do have time to walk around it at a leisurely pace."

I laugh. Today is our last day in Busan and my last day with Junho. He leaves Korea tomorrow and then I leave the day after that. Our dads are at the fish market, while we opted to spend the afternoon at the culture village. During the Korean War, many refugees fled to Busan and made makeshift houses on the hill. It was one of the poorest areas in Busan until it underwent a major renovation project, partnering with local artists to create the Gamcheon Culture Village of today. Now it is living, breathing art.

It feels fitting to be here with Junho. He grins at me as we make our way to the viewpoint, greeted by colorful rooftops and pastel walls.

We lean against the ledge, breathe it in.

"Hey," I say. "I just wanted to say sorry again for leaving you outside the flower shop. And for all the disappearing acts."

"You already apologized when you got back last night," Junho says.

"I know. But I'm not just talking about physically disappearing." I look out at the rooftops and then turn to face Junho. "I'm sorry for disappearing on you in other ways. Not telling you what's going on. Saying I'm fine when I'm not. My friend Nikita is always calling me out on that, saying I'm actually FINE in all caps when I say that—Falling Into Never-ending Emptiness."

He laughs. "Nikita and I would get along."

"I think so too." I fold my hands together, pressing them against my chest. "Anyway, truly, I'm sorry for all of that."

He's silent for a moment, taking it in. "I didn't want you to ever feel like you *had* to confide in me or anything, especially if you weren't ready to. But it did hurt sometimes when it felt like you were pushing me away. It's just . . . I like you a lot. I wanted to be with you."

Oh, Junho Kim. His words are so honest that it makes me blink back tears. There's no hiding with him, no pretending that everything is fine. I never thought in a million years that we'd go from standing outside a hoddeok stall as kids to this, to here. "I like you a lot too," I say.

He grins, and then his smile goes a little sad. "I just wish I could have been there for you when you were at your lowest. I felt so useless knowing you were going through something that I couldn't do anything about."

I survey his face. There are two Junhos that I've met so far. The first, dreamy and free, the one that simply wants to float in the Han River. The second, tense with the weight on his shoulders, the one who always has to make things right and keep the scales balanced in his family. There are two Junhos, but they're really one Junho, and I can see them both reflected in his eyes right now.

"You weren't useless," I say.

"Well, I definitely didn't do anything to make things better," he says, looking down at the ledge.

I smile at him. "You're someone who makes things better just by being there."

He looks up, surprised, his face turning pink. And then he looks at me, holding my eyes with his, soft and tender, and he leans in. I lean in too, closing my eyes. When our lips meet, I feel the kiss everywhere. In my fingertips, my toes, the depth of my stomach, every part of me. So this is what *here* feels like.

When we pull away, we're both smiling silly, like the couple of nerds we are. And then I remember.

"I have something for you!" I say, nudging his shoulder with mine.

"Oh?" He raises his eyebrows. "Is it another kiss?"

I laugh, reaching into my tote bag and pulling out the pocket-sized notebook with "My Brilliant Ideas" on the cover. I hold it out to him proudly. "For all your story ideas."

He looks touched. "You shouldn't have."

"I look forward to reading your webtoon one day."

"Actually, I did have one idea I've been meaning to tell you about." He looks nervous now, pressing the notebook between his hands. "It's kind of a collab project, like you suggested."

"With Zack?" I ask.

"No. I was actually thinking with you."

I blink. "With me?"

He nods. "I thought maybe we could write a story around Sensory Time Warp Syndrome. It doesn't have to be autobiographical or anything. But I feel like I don't see many stories about it, and it would be an important one to tell if you wanted to tell it."

I think about what Mr. Eunchul said at the Seoul meetup, how nobody cares about STWS anymore and we've all but faded into the background. Forums are nice, and so are articles and brochures, but a webtoon? Sharing a story through art? I imagine the possibilities, feeling the spark glow warm within me.

"That would be very cool," I say.

His whole face lights up, the way it does when he's excited. "Really? You're in?"

"Yeah! I would love to be part of that."

"Okay, but . . ." His face grows serious. "It would mean we'll have to keep in touch."

"Oh yeah?"

"Yeah. And probably FaceTime at least once a week."

"At least."

"Maybe even twice."

I nod, just as serious. "I think I can do that."

"It might require some in-person visits too. Possibly regular ones once you move out east."

I stick my hand out. "It'll be hard work, but deal."

He grins and shakes my hand, then turns it over and kisses my knuckles. Neither of us lets go, fingers intertwined as we leave the viewpoint and race down more alleys, the boy and the girl with the brilliant ideas.

That night, we head back to Gomo's place in Seoul. I didn't realize how much I missed her until I see her again. I hug her tight and she laughs, hugging me back.

"We're going to have to get you to visit soon, Nuna," Appa says. "We probably shouldn't let another ten years pass before we see each other again."

"It's about time," Gomo says. "I was just waiting for my invite!"

I decide now is a good time to give her the plum blossom banchan plate gift. She makes a properly big deal out of it, declaring it her favorite new dishware of all time. I also give Appa the mug since he's here and all. He inspects it carefully and then nods.

"Good," he says. "I'll use this."

From Appa, the highest of compliments.

The next morning—our last full day—I have an errand to run on my own before spending the rest of it with Appa and Gomo. I sit at my desk and write a letter, sealing it in an envelope, and then I head out to Hapjeong Station. Yoo Seri meets me there, backpack slung over her shoulders.

"Thanks so much for coming," I say.

"Of course. Thanks for emailing."

After my initial email to her about time loops, I also emailed again asking if she would be willing to come with me today to meet the Hapjeong Station Ghost. She agreed. We head down to the platform together, tapping our T-money cards to enter through the gate.

As we wait by the spot where he last appeared, I fill her in on my experience with time loops in Gwangju and Busan. "I have a theory about how people get stuck in time loops," I say. I've been thinking about this a lot since everything happened and I do my best now to put it into words. "For me, it was when I revisited a memory too many times in a row. But it wasn't just that. I feel like it also had to do with the fact that I *wanted* to go back. Like I was already mentally stuck in the past so my physical body just followed along, if that makes sense."

Seri nods, pulling out her phone to take notes. "That makes sense."

"I think time loops get stronger and more difficult to leave the longer you're in them," I continue. "So if it's true that the Hapjeong Station Ghost has been stuck in his memory since 2017, then it makes sense why he glitches so much."

"Interesting," Seri says, her thumbs flying across her phone screen. She glances at me. "It's amazing that you got out of your time loop. Not even once, but twice."

"Yeah." I still feel a cold sense of dread remembering how panicked I felt when I realized I was stuck. It was a claustrophobic feeling that I hope I never have to go through again.

"It makes you wonder what other rumors about time loops might be true," Seri says, looking grim. I think of Benji Grey-Diaz. "Or how many other people are lost in time loops that we just don't know about."

"Maybe that could be part of the app," I say. "A section where people can report missing loved ones who have STWS. Chances are they might be stuck in a time loop somewhere. And maybe once we get the word out there that time loops exist, missing person cases that were previously closed can be opened again."

"You might be onto something," Seri says.

We wait for an hour, two hours, then three. Eventually, I have to leave, but Seri promises to come back and check on the Hapjeong Station Ghost regularly. I give her the letter I wrote.

"I wanted to tell him about how I got stuck in a time

loop and how I got out," I say. "Even if he glitches back to the past, if you're able to pass this on to him, he should be able to read it in his memory."

"Got it," Seri says. "I'll also try to find out more about him so we can help bring him back. Maybe he has family members who are looking for him."

As I leave, the subway is about to pull in, and I pause to brush my fingers against the platform screen doors before they open. I remember what the ajusshi said right before he disappeared again. *It felt like this.*

I look down the tunnel and hope that wherever he is right now, he'll know the feeling of coming back home again soon.

I meet Appa and Gomo at the shijang. It is loud and bustling and I'm reminded again how much I'm going to miss this place. Seoul. Korea. All of it. I promise myself this isn't the last we'll see of each other.

Appa looks at ease, keeping pace with Gomo and weaving through the crowds like he's done this all his life. Which, in a way, I guess he has. He catches my eye and smiles. I smile back.

Things have been different between us since Busan. There's an understanding that wasn't there before. This morning, Gomo walked into the kitchen to find us both sitting there, eating bowls of cereal. We weren't talking much, but this time the silence wasn't distant. It was nice.

Afterward, we drifted off to do our own thing, because as much as we may enjoy each other's company now, we still like our alone time too.

I am my father's daughter.

We stop at a produce stall so Gomo can buy some pomegranates. I lift up my phone camera and take a picture. The pomegranates will make a nice background photo.

Out of the corner of my eye, I see a woman walking through the market with her two sons, holding their hands in each one of hers. I think of my mom, somewhere out there in Suwon, maybe walking with her sons through a marketplace just like this one. I'm still processing everything I learned about her over this trip and everything I remembered about her from the memories I visited. She had mood swings, she loved flowers, she was homesick, and she faced a lot of pressure to make impossibly big life decisions at a young age. I wonder if things could have been different for her, for us, if she didn't face so much stigma from her own culture and family when she needed them most.

Overwhelming hurt, anger, and sadness press against my chest, the way they always do when I think about her now. It's complicated. I know it'll take me a long time to process it all and I'm not sure I'll ever want to see her again knowing how she abandoned me, but I tuck the information that she's out there somewhere safely away in my mind. For one day.

I turn to Appa and see him watching the woman with

the two sons as well, and I can tell he's thinking about the same thing. For a moment, he's nineteen again, in love and full of hope for the future, unaware of what's to come.

Then he turns to me and smiles. "Ddeokbokki?"

"Ddeokbokki," I agree.

We go to eat.

Dear Mr. Hapjeong Station Ghost,

Did you know that's what people call you? It's true. There's even a webtoon about you, but it's not really about you. It's about a fictional gang of ghosts hunting for treasure in the Seoul subway lines so they can move on to the afterlife in peace. But that's not your story. Your story is about time loops.

Or at least, right now it is. I don't know if you know this, Ajusshi, but you are stuck in a time loop right now. That means you have been replaying the same memory over and over again since 2017. Maybe you're already aware of this, but I wanted to tell you just in case you're not because the first step is to know that it's real.

I was recently stuck in one myself. Not as long as you, but long enough that it scared me. For a minute, I thought maybe life would be better for me if I just stayed there. But then I saw my younger self and I knew I wanted to give her another chance to live her life, a whole and full life, outside of this bubble of a memory. I don't know if this is the way it works for everybody, but what helped me return was thinking about my dad. I had so many things I wanted to say to him that I knew I could only do in the present. Focusing on that and then actually being able to say all those things . . . it grounded me again.

I don't know why we return to certain memories. Maybe it's a sign that we haven't found closure in them. Maybe that's why sometimes we get stuck and the only way to get unstuck is to face it head-on.

I don't know if you believe in signs, and truthfully, I don't know if I do either. There are still lots of things I don't know. But what I do know is that the present is waiting for you, and I know this because it was waiting for me. It doesn't care that you disappear sometimes, even if it is for years. There's still a place for you here.

I hope you're able to return to it.

Sincerely,
Aimee Roh

Thirty

TWO MONTHS LATER

I stand at the developer, dropping my photo paper in and waiting for the image to appear. I'm in the darkroom working on my final project, a compilation of photos from spring break in Korea. It feels appropriate, looking back on my time in Korea here, in my sanctuary, my holy space.

The image appears slowly, black and white.

Snapshot: Appa and me posing with our ddeokbokki, sauce on our chins, smiles on our faces, Gomo's thumb in the corner of the picture from how she was holding the camera. I can almost hear the marketplace in the background. I call this one "family."

I'll be taking it to Montreal with me when I go to McGill in the fall. Originally, I wanted to leave Vancouver for university to get a fresh start, away from Appa and the silence that followed us. But by the time I chose which school I wanted to go to, it had nothing to do with what I was leaving behind. Instead, I made my choice based on the place I was most excited to have some new firsts. First time living in a new city, first time taking the train to Toronto to see Junho, first time having Appa come visit me and eating all the bagels in town, making new breakfast traditions.

My phone dings with a text. I finish the steps, moving the photo from the developer to the stop bath to the finish to the wash, before stepping out of the darkroom. I knock to make sure no one is coming in while I'm going out before stepping into the in-between room and then outside to the art studio.

I check my phone.

Appa:

Don't forget your appointment today. Here's the address in case you forgot.

He's sent me the details for my new therapist appointment today. They specialize in rare conditions like STWS. Nikita has offered to drive me, and afterward, we're going to IHOP for a full stack of pancakes and a side of hash browns so I can tell her all about the Vancouver STWS meetup I went to last week (no current film majors, future film directors this time) and she can tell me all about the new people she met at the UBC pre–first year mixers she's been attending.

I text back a thank-you and Appa sends me a thumbs-up. I scroll back to my other texts, looking at my message threads with Nikita and Junho and Gomo and even updates from Seri. For a long time, I thought that having STWS meant that I was alone. But these days, I've been feeling the opposite.

I may never stop disappearing completely, but for now I'm here. I inhale deep, lungs full, hope like honey melting on my tongue and the sun rising in my mind.

And that is enough for me.

Acknowledgments

First and foremost, thank you to Jennifer Ung, without whom this book wouldn't be a book at all. My favorite part of the process is when the story is just ours and we pass it back and forth, trying to tap into its potential and bring it to its fullest light. Thank you for believing it could get there and for guiding it every step of the way.

To Linda Epstein—what a journey, huh? Thank you for trusting in this story, but more than that, for trusting me and for being someone I can always rely on. Here's to the tears, the laughter, and the bibimbap bowls.

The brilliant artist behind the cover and design of this book is David Curtis. I am both grateful for and totally in awe of your creativity. Thank you also to Jessica White for your copyediting genius and for keeping my time zones in check. Truly, my deepest gratitude goes to the whole team at Quill Tree Books. It has been such an honor to work with you and to create together.

To all my friends and friendly faces in the book world— fellow writers, book bloggers, librarians, booksellers, and publishing pros. It is my joy to be part of this community with you. And to all my friends outside the book world who show up for me time and time again, thank you. Love you.

A special shout-out to Graci Kim, Jessica Kim, Susan Lee, and Grace Shim. You know that classic umbrella scene in K-dramas? To me, the Kimchingoos are that umbrella: protection from the rain and proof of love.

Special shout-out as well to Sarah Harrington, Grace Li, and Carly Whetter. I would choose the seat by the window every time for you three. A toast to everything we've celebrated and all our celebrations to come!

To my family, the ones who make life what it is—아빠, 엄마, 언니, 오빠, John, and 세연언니. Thank you for being my biggest supporters. To Emory, Jonah, and Chloe, I love you in the chaos and I love you in the calm. You make my world so much brighter.

To Sue O. 사랑해, 사랑해요, 사랑합니다. To be read in the Mickey Mouse voice.

And lastly, to you, reader—this book means a lot to me, and it is my greatest hope that it might mean something to you too. Thank you, thank you, and thank you again, always.